Where's the Harm?

Where's the Harm?

Gillian Roberts

Five Star
Unity, Maine

Five Star Mystery
Published in conjunction with Tekno Books and Ed Gorman.

Cover photograph by Randy Pamphrey

September 1999

First Edition

Five Star Standard Print Mystery Series.

The text of this edition is unabridged.

Set in 11 pt. Plantin by Rick Gundberg.

Printed in the United States on permanent paper.

Library of Congress Cataloging-in-Publication Data

Roberts, Gillian.
    Where's the harm? / by Gillian Roberts — 1st ed.
      p.   cm. — (Five Star mystery series)
    Contents: Hog heaven — Fury duty — What's a woman to do? — One beautiful body — Goodbye, Sue Ellen — The shrine of Eleanor — Where's the harm in that? — Love is a many-splintered thing — Let this be a lesson — After happily ever — Clear sailing — Heart break.
    ISBN 0-7862-2036-8 (hc : alk. paper)
    1. Detective and mystery stories, American. I. Title. II. Series.
PS3557.R356W44   1999
813´.54—DC21   99-31278

Table of Contents

HOG HEAVEN

Harry Towers walked out of his office building and blinked in the late-afternoon light. The sea of homebound bodies divided around him as he deliberated how, and with whom, to fill the hours ahead.

The redheaded receptionist had other plans. Lucy, his usual standby, had run off to Vegas with a greeting-card salesman. Charlene was back with her husband, at least for tonight. Might as well check out Duffy's.

He stood a little straighter, smoothed his hair over his bald spot, and sucked in his stomach. Duffy's was a giant corral into which the whole herd of thirty-plus panic-stricken single women stampeded at nightfall. Duffy's Desperates, he called them. Not prime stock, but all the same, the roundup saved time.

He walked briskly. Everything would be fine. He didn't need that stupid redheaded receptionist.

"Harry? Harry Towers?"

The sidewalks were still crowded, but Harry spotted the owner of the melodic voice so easily, it was as if nobody but the two of them were on the streets.

He had seen her a few times before, recently, right around this time of day. She was the blonde, voluptuous kind you had to notice. A glossy sort of woman, somebody you see in magazines or on TV. Not all that young, not a baby, but not a

7

bimbo. And definitely not a Duffy's Desperate.

She repeated his name and continued moving resolutely toward him. He tried not to gape.

"You *are* Harry Towers, aren't you?" A small, worried frown marred her perfect face.

He smiled and nodded, straightening up to his full height. He was a tall man, but her turquoise eyes were on a level with his.

"I thought so!" Her face relaxed in a wide smile. "Remember me?" Her voice was so creamy, he wanted to lick it.

"I . . . well—" In his forty-five years, he had never before laid eyes on this woman, except for the sidewalk glimpses this week. Harry did not pay a whole lot of the remembering kind of attention to most women, but this was not most women. This one you'd remember even if you had Alzheimer's.

She was using the old don't-I-know-you-from-somewhere? line, and it amused him. She'd even gone to the trouble to find out his name. Flattering, to say the least.

"Does the name Leigh Endicott sound familiar?" she prompted.

"Oh!" he said emphatically, nodding, playing the game. "Leigh . . . Endicott. Sure . . . now I—well, it must be—"

"Years," she said with one of those woeful smiles women give when they talk about time. "Even though it seems like yesterday." She shook her head, as if to clear away the time in between. "I've thought about you so often, wondered what became of you." She put her hand on his sleeve, tenderly.

If only the redhead hadn't left the building before him—if only she could see him now!

"I always hoped I'd find you again someday," she purred.

She was overdoing it. Should he tell her to skip the old-friend business? They didn't need a make-believe history. He decided to keep quiet, not rock the boat, follow her lead.

"Why don't we find someplace comfortable?" he said. "To, uh, reminisce?"

She glanced at her watch, then shrugged and smiled at him, nodding.

"There's a place around the corner," he said. "Duffy's." The Desperates would shrivel up and turn to dust when they saw this one. Then they'd know, all those self-important spritzer drinkers, that Harry Towers still had it. All of it.

They started walking, her arm linked through his. Suddenly, she stopped short. "I just had a wonderful idea. I have a dear little farmhouse in the country. Very peaceful and private. Would you mind skipping the bar? I'm sure it's too noisy and crowded for a really good . . . talk. My car's over there. I can drive you back later—if you feel like leaving."

What a woman! Right to the point! He hated the preliminaries, the song-and-dance routine, anyway. He followed her to the parking lot, grinning.

I am in hog heaven, he thought. *Hog heaven.*

The ride was a timeless blur. Harry was awash, drowning in the mixed perfumes of the car's leather, the spring evening, the woman beside him, and the anticipation of the hours ahead. When Leigh spoke, her voice, rich and sensuous, floated around him. He had to force himself to listen to the words instead of letting them tickle his pores and ruffle his hair.

"Almost there, Harry," she was saying. "Don't you love this area? Open country. Free. Natural. I love the farmhouses, the space . . ."

Almost there. Free. Natural. Wonderful words.

Leigh, eyes still on the road, voice talking about the wonders of the countryside, placed a manicured hand on his thigh.

God? He said silently, needing the Deity for the first time in years. God, let this really be happening.

After dinner she sent Harry into the living room. "Make yourself comfortable," she insisted, "while I clean up. I'll bring in coffee." No number about sharing the work. He couldn't believe his luck.

The tape stopped, and he picked out a mellow one. Make-out music, they called it a century or two ago when he was young. Why did that seem so funny? He stifled a giggle. He turned the volume to a soft, inviting level, then settled into the rich velvet sofa. He felt a little weird. Almost like a teenager again, that racing high, that thrumming excitement.

What a woman! He couldn't believe his luck. He stretched and enjoyed the memory of the meal. Her own recipe, her own invention. Spicy, delicious, exotic. Like Leigh herself, like the charged talk that had hovered around the table, like the possibilities of a long night in the remote countryside.

"Here you are," she announced, carrying a tray with a coffeepot, creamer, sugar bowl and cups. She bent close and his giddy light-headedness, the speeding double-time rush of blood through his veins, intensified.

She poured the coffee, then stepped back and spread her arms as if to embrace the room. "Do you like my place?" she asked. "The people at work think I'm crazy to be this isolated, this far from everything. But I love my privacy. Or maybe I like animals better than people." She laughed. "Present company excluded, of course."

Bubbles of excitement popped in Harry's veins. "Have a seat," he suggested, patting the sofa next to him. He wiggled his lips. They felt thick, a little foreign and tingly. Stupid to have eaten so much. And all that wine, too. Now he was bloated, sluggish.

Leigh, on the other hand, seemed wired. "This is a working farm," she said. "Cows, pigs, horses. There's a caretaker, of course." She stopped her pacing. "But don't worry—he won't bother us. He's all the way on the other side of the property, and anyway, he's away for the night."

"Leigh—" he began. He sounded whiny and stopped himself. But all the same, why couldn't they start enjoying this nice private place before her stupid roosters crowed? He was reminded of his teens, of dates with nervous girls chattering furiously to keep his attention—and hands—off their bodies. It had annoyed him even then. He decided to see if actions would speak louder than words, and smacked at the sofa's velvet.

It worked. She finally sat down. But just out of easy reach.

He felt planted in the soft cushions. He took a moment to evaluate the pros and cons of uprooting himself.

"Do you know which is the most intelligent barnyard animal?" she asked.

Who cared? Frankly, even a brainless chicken was beginning to seem brighter than this woman. Didn't she remember why they were here?

She refilled his coffee cup. He sipped at it while he tried to figure a way to change the subject.

"Pigs," she said. "It's almost a curse on them, being that smart. They know when they're going to slaughter. They scream and fight and try to prevent their own destruction."

Harry finished the coffee. There was no subtle way to stop her, so he'd be direct. "I don't care about pigs," he said emphatically. "I care about you. Come closer."

"I'm fond of pigs." She stayed in place. "Don't you care about what I care about? About who I am?"

"Of course! I didn't mean to . . ." Damn. She was one of those. He hadn't expected it, from the way she'd come on to him, but she was one more of them who needed to discuss their innermost feelings first, get to know the man, make things serious and important.

"Let's take things slowly," she said. "I've waited years and years to be with you again."

"Ah, c'mon," he said. "We're adults. Don't pretend anymore. I like you, you like me. Tha's enough. Don't need games."

She refilled his cup, then held it out to him.

He stared at her hands, confused.

"Games can be fun, Harry," she murmured. "And so can the prizes at the end." She put the cup in his hands.

It required a great deal of effort to bring it to his lips.

"You still haven't answered the first question, you know," she said with a small smile.

He shook his head. He had no idea what she was talking about. "I really don't like games," he said. The whole idea made him tired.

"Yes, you do." Her voice was a croon, a lullaby. "Sure you do. I know that about you. You just like the game to be yours, the old familiar one. But this one is new. This is mine, and it's called 'Do You Remember Me?' "

She was all smiles and burbles, and he felt suddenly chilled.

"Oh, you look puzzled," she said. "I'll give you a clue." She stood up. *"Campus."* She clicked musically, sounding like a game-show timer.

"College?" he asked, frowning. "State?"

"Good!" She waited. "Any more? Who am I, Harry Towers? You have fifteen seconds." She began her manic clicking noise again.

"You were there?" His voice sounded remote and dislocated, as it weren't coming out of his own throat.

12

She nodded pertly. "A freshman when you were a junior. Think." He was afraid she would begin her timer again, but instead she asked him if he wanted brandy.

He shook his head. "Feel a little . . ." He clutched the arm of the sofa for support.

She nodded. "So, how are we doing with those clues?"

"I . . ." He said her name silently, hoping it would connect with something, but all it did was bang from side to side in his brain. Leeleeleelee . . . a sharp bell tolling painfully.

"Ahhh," she said, "so you really don't remember me. How about that."

He couldn't think of what he should say. She was all snap-and-crackle confusion, and he was fuzzy lint. "Sorry," he whispered. Actually, he decided, she wasn't worth it. Too much time and effort. As soon as he felt a little better, he wanted out.

"Harry," she whispered. "Your mouth is open. You're drooling."

He tried to close it.

"I guess it would be hard to remember one girl out of that crowd of them you had." She smiled down at him, and he felt the tension ease.

There had been so many girls sticking to him as if he were made of Velcro. Such a good time. While it lasted. He wondered where his old letter sweater was, whether it still fit him, then remembered he was supposed to be trying to remember Leigh. But the girls were one big blur of sweet-smelling hair, firm breasts, lips, assorted parts.

She sat down so close to him that her perfume increased his dizziness. "Poor baby," she crooned. "You're woozy. Rest your head in my lap."

She stroked his thinning hair as if she loved every strand.

13

Beneath her hand, his head swirled and popped, as the dinner wine and spices fermented. Maybe she wasn't such a bitch. He couldn't get a fix on her. Maybe it was good she liked the sound of her own voice too much. He needed time. She'd been at State with him. He rummaged again through his memories of all those girls, those legs and arms and shiny hair. Which one had been Leigh? He couldn't remember any of them. Female faces had a way of blurring away by the next morning, let alone after decades.

"Innasorority?" he said in a soft hiss.

She shook her head. "I was so shy. A loner. Until Harry Towers invited me to his fraternity party and everything was magically changed."

Which party? No way to separate out those drunken, sweaty, wonderful nights. God, but those guys were fun. So many laughs. Best years of his life.

"Except that I never saw you again," Leigh said.

"Musta been outa my mind," he gasped chivalrously. Maybe it would appease her.

She chuckled very softly. "Wish you hadn't been. You can't imagine what a difference it would have made to me if you'd asked me out again."

So he hadn't been the most steady guy. That's how he was, who he was. But he'd never been a fool, so why hadn't he seen as much of this one as possible? Had something happened? Damn, but the memory slate was clean. Not even a chalk smear on it. He tried to sit up, to face her, to say something, but he only made it halfway.

Abruptly, she stood. He flopped down on the cushions, then grabbed the back of the sofa and tried to pull into a sitting position.

She was going into the bedroom. Maybe talking time was over, just like that. Maybe they weren't going to have to deal with ancient history and guessing games, after all. He staggered to his feet.

"No. Stay," she called out. "I need something."

Safe sex, he realized. Sure. Okay. His legs wobbled and he couldn't stop swaying. He sank back into the sofa.

She returned and handed him a ragged-edged snapshot.

"Whadoss . . ." He gave up the effort of asking what this had to do with anything.

"It's part of the game," she said. "The last clue."

He focused his eyes with difficulty. When he had managed the feat, he regretted the effort. The girl in the photograph had a moonshaped face with dark hair pulled back severely so that her ears stuck out like flaps. Sunlight bounced off her glasses, emphasizing the shadows cast by her enormous nose, her chubby cheeks, and her collection of chins. For no reason Harry could think of, she was smiling, revealing teeth that gaped like pickets on a wobbly fence. A real loser. A dog. A pig. Harry let the picture drop onto the coffee table.

"Too bad," she said. "We're out of time. Ladies and gentlemen, our contestant has forfeited the game. But don't turn off that set—we've got a few surprises left! It's not over till it's over!" She loomed above him, a giantess. Then she pushed the picture back in front of him. "Harry Towers, meet Leigh Endicott," she said.

"Wha?" He had an overwhelming sense of wrongness. His mouth was painfully dry. He reached toward the coffee, but his fingers weren't working properly. He sat, arms hanging loose, staring at the old black-and-white snapshot on the table.

"How could you not recognize me?" Her voice was sweet and coquettish. "The only changes have been time—oh, and a few superficial adjustments, like a diet, a nose bob, contact lenses, ear pinning, chin enlarging, straightening and capping the teeth and bleaching the hair. Nothing compared to what's possible nowadays. But that was a long time ago."

A whoosh came out of the hollowness inside Harry. He'd taken her—that photo girl—to a party. He felt chilly, then hot. Something wanted to be remembered. Something hovered just above his head, ready to fall.

"I left school to earn the money for the changes," she said. "Took me four years, same as my degree would have." She walked toward the window. "Only thing is, at the end I was still the same girl inside, but who cares about that, right?"

He put up his hand like a traffic cop, to stop her words from falling on his skull. He was cold again, afraid, needed to explain and defend himself, as if he were on trial, but when he opened his mouth, he gagged. When was it? Why? Did he really remember certain times . . . ? Why did Duffy's Desperates suddenly stampede into his mind in a great cloud of dust?

"Your party," she said. "My first date on campus. My first date, actually. I had such a good time. Every little girl knows the story of Cinderella—why shouldn't it happen to all of us? And Prince Charming had nothing on you, Harry. But when I left the room to powder my oversized nose, I overheard two of your darling fraternity brothers. Very drunk and very happy fraternity brothers. They were laughing so much, I could barely make out the joke, except that they kept repeating one particular word. This is the last question in the game, Harry. Do you know the word?"

His heart was going to explode. Party—ugly girl. Laughing. It all connected, turned fiery and molten. Pig. Pig party. Had forgotten all about them. Probably didn't have them anymore. Defunct, part of the world of the dinosaurs, but back then . . .

"Weren't supposed to know . . ." he said. "Just a . . .

prank. Fun. No harm meant."

She loomed over him, stony and enormous. A warrior woman.

"F'give," he begged. "Boys will be . . ." What? What will boys be? What did he mean? Now or then—what? His mind was falling apart, great chunks slopping like mud into heaps. His hands were damp and cold. He tried to smile, although his mouth had become enormous, like a clown's, and rubbery.

"Stop groveling," she said. "There's no point. Or do you still think we're here because I *yearn* for you?" She laughed harshly but with real amusement.

He was freezing. His hands trembled uncontrollably, even while they lay in place.

She waved her arms at her imaginary audience, somewhere outside the windows. "The game is over, folks. Over," she said. Then she turned back to Harry. "You thought you caught a dream tonight, didn't you?" she said. "Maybe I'd make up for everybody else's indifference, would see past the sad slick of failure you wear like skin, past your dead-end job, your saggy gut, your stupid life, your smell of loneliness. You wanted me to find the real you—the special person inside, didn't you?"

Her voice was low and cool, only distantly interested in him, as if he were a specimen. He wished she would scream, maybe blot out the deafening sound of his own pulse.

"I understand it all, Harry," she said, "because that's what I wanted, what I believed, too, the night you asked me to your party. And get this: Neither of us—not me years ago, not you tonight—understood one damn thing that was going on."

His head ached as if she'd physically beaten him.

"I found out accidentally," she said. "You're going to find out very deliberately. That's the only difference." She walked away. "Pig party," she said. "Where all you perfect, self-important fraternity jackasses could observe and be amused by a freak show of imperfect but oblivious females. How side-splitting of us to think we were actual dates, actual lovable, desirable humans! What fun it must have been to wink and poke each other in the ribs, award the man who'd found the absolute worst, laugh through the night about us. It's quite an experience, Harry, finding out you're a laughing matter. Changes a person forever."

He had to get the hell out of here, but his limbs were bone-less; he couldn't stand.

"Of course, it was also a learning experience," she said. "A chance to grow. For years now I've wanted you to share it, have the same chance, but I don't belong to a fraternity and besides, I'd like to think there aren't any more pig parties. So I had to find a way to return the favor personally." She came very close, kneeled in front of him.

A wave of nausea engulfed him. He swallowed hard and struggled to get to his feet.

"You're not going anywhere!" she snapped, pushing him back in place with one hand. "Do you really think it's the wine, or a few peppers making you feel so rotten? Aren't you worried?"

His burning eyes opened wide. "Poison?" he gasped.

She smiled. "It's a possibility, isn't it? I've had years to prepare for tonight. But why be concerned? This is a party, Harry. Your very own pig party. In fact, my dear, you *are* the party—the pig's party."

He nearly wept from the sawtooth edge of screams slicing the edges of his mind.

"The pigs behind the house, remember? Poor babies, they can't enjoy the miracles of cosmetic surgery. They're stuck as pigs forever, so surely they're entitled to a little piggy treat

18

now and then. You'll give them such pleasure."

"Hhhhh?"

"How?" Her voice traveled from a great distance and echoed through him, down to his fingertips.

"They eat almost anything, of course. But you—you'll be the best dish they ever had. Of course, we won't let them have all of you, will we? Nobody's ever had that. We'll do it bit by bit. Start with gourmet tidbits. The, uh, choice cuts, shall we say? The sought-after, prized, yummy parts."

Tears dribbled from his eyes.

"You know what they call pig food? Slops, Harry. How appropriate."

He heard dreadful, guttural sounds.

"Be still," she said. "And your nose is running. How disgusting."

He was small and lost and terrified, poisoned and paralyzed on a velvet sofa, about to be butchered, to have pigs eat his—pigs swallow his—

He summoned all of his strength, determined to get free. But his knees buckled and he dropped to the floor. "Please," he said between sobs, "was so long ago . . ."

"Not long enough," she said. "I realized that two weeks ago, when I saw you downtown. My jolt of pain wasn't old or faded. Some things are forever. You killed a part of me that night. However plain or fat or shy I was, I had an innocent pride and dignity, and you took it away. You turned me into a pig."

He howled at the top of his lungs.

"Hush. Nobody can hear," she reminded him. "Nobody knows you're here. For that matter, nobody knows *I'm* here. This isn't my house—it's a friend's, and he's away. So is the caretaker." She walked around him. "And for the record, my married name isn't Leigh Endicott. Anyway, we're both

19

going to simply disappear from here. But you'll do it bit by bit." She paused in an exaggerated pose of thought. "Or should we say bite by bite?" she asked with a grin.

He crawled, crying. An inch. No more.

"Why struggle so?" she said. "You are, quite literally, dead meat. On the other hand, you're about to be reborn, to give of yourself at last, to become whole—swine, inside and out."

The door was impossibly far away. He sprawled, numb and exhausted, gasping as the dark closed in. He could feel himself begin to die at the edges. His fingers were already gone, and his feet.

Through static and splutters and whirs in his brain, he heard her move around, run water, open cabinets.

"All clean now," she said. "Not a trace." She leaned down and pulled up one of his eyelids. "Tsk, tsk," she said. "Look what's become of the big, bad wolf."

He dissolved into a shapeless, quivering stain on the floor. All his mind could see was a pig, heavy and bloated, pushing its hideous, hairy snout into its trough, into the slops, grunting with pleasure as it ate . . . him.

Glass broke, a door slammed, but all Harry heard was a fat sow's squeal of pleasure as it chewed and smacked and swallowed . . . him.

He felt a hand on his shoulder. He gasped, ran his own hands over his body once, then twice. Everything was there. He was intact and whole! He burst into tears.

"Damn drunk. Probably a junkie," a voice said. "Breaks in to use the place as a toilet. Jesus." Harry was pulled to his feet by men with badges. Police.

"Listen, I—" he began. His head hurt.

"You have the right to remain silent," the taller man began. He droned through his memorized piece. Harry couldn't believe it. They searched him and looked disappointed when they found nothing. "Passed out before you could take anything," the taller man said.

"But I wasn't—" They weren't interested. He told them about Leigh. They ignored him. He found out that an anonymous caller—female—had alerted the police to a prowler on the farm. He told them they had it all wrong, that it was her, Leigh Somebody who'd picked him up, taken him here, drugged him, smashed the window so it'd look like he'd broken in, and called them, setting him up. He explained it to them, to the lawyer they appointed, to the psychiatrist, to the technician who analyzed the drugs in his bloodstream—street drugs they were, nothing fancy or traceable, damn the woman. He explained it to the judge. Nobody listened or believed or cared.

He stopped explaining. He endured the small jail until they released him. He paid for the broken window and the soiled rug. Paid the fine for trespassing, for breaking and entering. Paid through the nose for a taxi back to the city and his apartment.

In his mailbox, the only personal mail was a heart-shaped card with a picture of two enormous pigs nuzzling each other. He burned it.

From that day on, Harry's Towers' stoop became more pronounced. He no longer combed his hair over his bald spot or sucked in his stomach. He stayed home nights, watching television alone.

And he never ate bacon or pork chops or ham steaks, for they, along with many other former delights, tasted like ashes in his mouth.

FURY DUTY

It wasn't my favorite night even before Celia became the bearer of bad news.

I was already failing to cope with several other problems.

Item: all the sinks in the house were backed up and the plumber's estimate was twice my bank balance.

Item: my dog had impregnated a hapless bitch whose owner demanded that I harvest Fido's wild oats.

Major item: the manuscript my editor expected in two days had no ending. Actually, there was an obligatory final scene. All impediments removed, my couple would marry. That is generally considered a happy ending, although I can't imagine why. Nonetheless, my problem was how to get my characters to the altar without retracing paths taken in my earlier books.

I write both romance and horror novels. They aren't all that different, when you think about it, so I considered solving my problem by switching genres. My hero could become a werewolf. I'd make him look like my passionate dog and then I'd kill him off.

My women's group was due in a matter of minutes, and I slapped icing on a mess of cake that I'd been too rushed to leave in the oven long enough. I decided that *Sweet Savage Steppes* shouldn't be about werewolves. Maybe its brooding Slavic hero—thank heavens for glasnost!—was sufficiently unique. Mikhail could say and do the exact same thing an Iowa farmer did in my last book and nobody would notice.

The cake looked like a relief map of Switzerland. Once upon a time, when cooking was still a female form of arm wrestling, this would have caused an anxiety attack. But my women's group had been around too long to have its members lose face through mediocre handling of flour and sugar.

The group started at the dawn of time, the era before the ERA, to coin a phrase. We were all married then, and if we wanted to get out at night without husbands, it was cooking lessons, a Tupperware party, or a book club. We chose books—with a little food on the side.

When we first began, we ate fruit suspended in Jell-O and talked about best-sellers, babies, color schemes and couples. Later, we ate whole grains, read feminist tracts and talked about ourselves. Most recently, everybody went on her own special diet, read only business and professional articles (or in my case, my alter ego, Alexa Fury's romantic gush) and talked about disappointments—children, jobs, sex and husbands, our own exes and the recycled ones we date.

In just a few minutes, we were going to eat undercooked cake and discuss an obscure South American novel I hadn't had time to open, thanks to the miseries of Mikhail and Ariel.

I began cleaning up, but before I'd made a dent, the doorbell rang. My premature guest was Celia Arnold, toting the veggies and low-cal dip she always brings. Celia has spent the last twenty-five years trying to lose ten, then twenty, now thirty pounds.

"Something horrible's happened, Dee," she said, plunking her vegetables onto the kitchen table. "I saw the archfornicator."

"Who?" Hard to believe, but I thought she meant a guy—an intriguing-sounding one at that.

"The netsuke—Laurel's netsuke! The one with the woman and three men. You always talked about it!"

Automatically, I looked out the kitchen window toward the charred remains of the house where Laurel Tobias once lived. It's been on the market for two years now. Nobody wants the half-burned scene of a murder.

Maybe you've read about Jackson Tobias? The man who shot his estranged wife so he could get their valuable collection of Japanese carvings? He'd bashed in a cabinet to get the figures, and he tried to hide the fact by burning the house and the cabinet to cinders, but I saw the fire and reported it in time for the evidence of his crime to still be intact.

They only found one netsuke—in his apartment. He insisted Laurel had given it to him a week earlier. The same night he'd given her his gun to ease her fears. He said. Everybody knew he'd taken all the netsukes and hidden them.

Except now two years later, Celia had found a second netsuke.

"Jackson's in prison," I said. "He must have an accomplice selling off the pieces. Maybe that redheaded tramp he was seeing?"

Celia sat down on a kitchen chair. "Wrong," she whispered.

"Cut the drama, would you?" I heard a wet plop as icing slopped off my ski slope of a cake. Why we served desserts when everybody wanted to lose weight escaped me. I glared at the cake, but it did no good, so I scowled instead at Celia.

"I saw it last week," she said. "At an Open Spaces meeting. The hostess heard me gasp and thought I was a prude. She rushed to explain that netsukes were used by the Japanese to close their money bags, that this one was centuries old, ivory and very finely carved. Actually, we had a lot of fun checking exactly what each of the three men was doing to

24

that woman. Did you ever realize that one of them was—"

"Celia, get to the point!"

"Okay. The fornicator was a fiftieth birthday gift to her husband. From a cousin, a year ago. I couldn't figure out how. I mean Jackson was arrested two years ago, the morning after he—the morning after the fire."

I kept my hands steady spooning decaf into the coffee maker.

Celia twiddled a carrot stick. "It made me sick to think of him making a profit from murder. Besides, any netsuke money belongs to Laurel's estate, not his."

Maybe. The dispute had never been settled. Laurel had claimed that her father, a merchant seaman, collected the netsukes years earlier. Jackson insisted he'd bought them on his own travels. Whatever.

"I told this woman I was a collector and I'd never seen one like this."

Next to my ex-husband, Celia is the worst storyteller I know. "Yes, yes," I prompted. "Did she know *where* the cousin found the figure?" Maybe pornographic money-bag closers had been a Japanese fad two hundred years ago. Maybe there are thousands of teeny tiny orgy carvings. Maybe that woman owned somebody else's archfornicator.

Celia pouted. I was spoiling all her fun.

"The group'll be here any minute," I said, to placate her.

She sighed loudly. "I called the cousin and *finally,* he gave me the name of a dealer. I think maybe this guy is not completely on the up-and-up."

"The cousin?"

"The art dealer. How would I know about the cousin? I never even met—"

"Celia!"

"I left twelve messages in four days before the dealer returned my call. He gave me the name of an auction house. Where I again left message after message."

"You should have called me. I would have found ways to speed things up."

"You always take charge. I wanted to do this myself."

The coffee maker made the bubbling digestive noises I generally find comforting, but this time they weren't enough.

"The auction house was in Chicago, Dee. *Chicago*. Why? There are places here in town." She leaned closer. "I drove there today because they wouldn't talk on the phone. But when I marched in and said I had questions to do with a dead friend and that maybe I'd call the police, they came around. I was so scared! What if they'd really made me call the cops!"

"Celia? The records?"

"They told me who'd brought in the figures. *Figures*, Dee, not just one. Two dozen netsukes." She leaned back and smiled smugly.

"You're driving me crazy."

"Okay. They were brought in *two years ago*. In October. One entire month before Laurel died. And they were brought in by a woman." Her smile faded. "I've been sick since I heard. We've done a terrible thing! Jackson didn't steal anything that night, and if Jackson didn't steal anything, then maybe he didn't—"

I stood up, too charged to stay in place. "Don't rush to conclusions. First of all, you said two dozen pieces, but Laurel had over thirty. What about the rest?"

"Maybe she placed her figures at more than one auction house."

"Second, we could be talking about somebody else altogether, not Laurel. Somebody else could have owned an archfornicator as part of a collection. Did the auctioneer tell you the name of the woman who sold them?"

Celia nodded.

"*Yes?* Well?"

"You'll never guess."

I resisted the urge to bang her infuriating head against the wall.

"It wasn't Laurel Tobias," Celia finally said.

"Then this whole thing is a tempest in a—"

"Erin S. Tisiphone brought them in."

I gasped. It had been a joke among the three of us. Way back, when our consciousnesses were rising, husbands fled. Mine packed and departed first. Celia's waited, then took off with their baby-sitter, who, he claimed, was still "a real woman."

Jackson seemed to believe this was a phase we were going through, and he didn't budge. Instead, he labeled us "The Three Furies." In fact, that's how I acquired my pen name. Deedee Blatt isn't either romantic or horrifying, so I became Alexa—as close as I could come to Alecto the Implacable—Fury. In the wake of the womanly baby-sitter, Celia picked Megaera, the Jealous One, and the meek Laurel accepted third and last choice, Tisiphone, the Avenger of Blood. But it was a mouthful, so she played with the Greek name for the Furies, *Erinyes,* and became Erin S.

"What'll we do?" Celia wailed. "We testified that the netsukes were in her house, which meant that Jackson stole them. We convicted him."

"The cabinet, remember? It was smashed."

Celia shrugged. "Maybe she did it. Maybe she was angry, or it was a coincidence, an accident, or somebody else altogether murdered her."

"With Jackson's gun?" I shook my head. "And who else

had a key? There wasn't any break-in, and the door was locked."

"She killed herself," Celia said. "He probably really did give his gun to her, like he said. We thought she told us everything, but she didn't. We didn't know she'd sold the netsukes. Why didn't she tell us she needed money instead of going all the way to Chicago out of shame?"

"Maybe that wasn't why she went." I spoke slowly and deliberately. "Everything makes sense if Laurel wanted to frame Jackson. Make her suicide look like murder. And maybe Erin S. Tisiphone was a message for us if we ever found out—to remember friends and Furies and not go soft."

Celia's normally pink skin blanched. "But even so, if Jackson didn't do it—what did we do?"

We had done plenty. Celia and I had testified on behalf of Laurel. And the entire book group had taken off from work and gone to court every single day to sit like a second, silent jury, condemning Jackson Tobias. The fact is, we convicted the man. The fact is, he deserved it.

But now Celia seemed ready to run to the police and recant. I had to talk her out of making a terrible mistake, but there was no time or opportunity, because the bell rang.

"The women!" Celia said. "They'll know what to do. After all," she asked plaintively, "what are friends for?"

Typically, Celia took forever retelling her story, but for once, I was grateful, because it gave me time to think. By the time she was near the close, we were deeply into the evening, finished with lasagna and salad, through everybody's decision to cheat on their diets "just this once" and into friendly reassurances that my cake was okay. "Pudding-ish, but more delicious than it looks—like us," someone quipped. Women of a certain age make jokes.

We sat in a homey, rough circle in the living room. It gave me pleasure to watch the firelight flicker over the timeworn faces. It had been hard as hell keeping this house after my divorce, but when my friends gathered in it, it seemed well worth it.

When Celia finally stopped, there was a chorus of reactions. Nobody was overly shocked that depressed Laurel had committed suicide, only that she had made her own death look like murder. I listened to the exclamations. "Timid Laurel framed her husband!" "Who would have thought that of her?" "It's hard to believe that Jackson's innocent."

I recognized my clue. "Maybe Jackson isn't innocent," I said. "Even if he isn't guilty of pulling the trigger or stealing the netsukes."

"I hate word games." Janet, the newest member, was young enough and still-married enough to believe in absolutes. "Either Jackson Tobias killed his wife or he didn't."

I gentled them toward the idea. "Perhaps the question is *when* he killed her, not whether." I waited until they'd absorbed that, then I continued. "Since there are so many ways to destroy someone, and so many steps to the process, why only be concerned with the last one—the issue of whose finger pulled the trigger or lit that match? Why do we endlessly debate when life begins and never consider when death begins?"

"What are you getting at, Dee?"

"There are more crimes than there are laws. Surprising as Celia's discovery may be, I think the issue is not whether Jackson shot Laurel, but whether he murdered her."

The firelight played against the walls while the women digested my cake and my words.

"Listen, we're"—Janet counted—"twelve ordinary women who—"

"A jury," another woman said. "We're a jury."

"Not really. We aren't the law." Janet was so disgustingly young and sincere, I had been against admitting her, and now I was convinced I'd been right.

"There are lots of systems of law," a woman who'd been part of the group all twenty-five years said. "Erin S. Tisiphone is a reminder that the furies had their own ways of handling injustice."

There was as long silence. I refilled coffee cups and wineglasses and watched our shadows paint the walls.

"I say we put Jackson back on trial," someone finally decided. "Tonight. Here. Now."

"For what, precisely?" Janet snapped. She was feisty, I'll give her that. Eleven women versus her, and she held her ground.

"For murder. By legal methods."

One woman hunched over her coffee cup, as if seeing visions in it. "Like, do you remember when she was finally able to stop helping—for no pay—with the business and the kids were launched and she went back to her painting? How he said that only immature children deluded themselves about their so-called talent."

"How about," a second voice added, "when she had her first show and he bought all her work before the opening—to spare her humiliation, he said?"

"And then never hung a one of them up," Celia murmured.

"He was so stingy. She made the girls' clothing and Halloween costumes and the curtains and drapes and could barely afford paintbrushes while he whooped it up on business expenses and—"

"Remember his white-glove inspections? And jokes about wishing he could afford the servants Laurel so obviously needed?"

"I'm not sure I like where this is going!" Janet said. "You're talking about leaving an innocent man in prison."

"Not forever. He's in for manslaughter and you watch—he'll be out in seven years."

"Which is a shorter sentence than Laurel served!"

"But still!" Even in the flickering light, I could see Janet's jaw set in righteous indignation. "You don't imprison a man because of an unpleasant domestic life or—"

"We're talking about justice," someone countered. "The man eroded her self-esteem, broke her spirit and destroyed her before she put a gun into her mouth. *That isn't innocence!*"

"You didn't know him, Janet," an older member said. "You didn't know her, either. You never saw any of it."

"Like how, whenever she said anything, he'd get a patient, patronizing expression, like she was a cute but stupid pet."

"Or how about the food? In front of whoever was there—clients, his friends, us—he'd poke his fork, purse his lips, question ingredients, apologize to guests, saying poor Laurel had tried so hard and he was so proud, anyway. She withered in front of our eyes."

"Once, when I was away on vacation and Laurel thought Jackson was away on business, I saw him and a young woman in a very unbusinesslike embrace."

"Well, I saw him right here in town with a real bimbo—wild red hair and skirt that looked painted on, and that was the same day Laurel was—the day she died! It was disgusting how they were carrying on. Poor Laurel, hoping and hoping he'd come back. I'm glad Dee convinced me not to tell Laurel right away or I'd feel responsible for her suicide, now that I think of it."

"Jackson once came on to me," a new voice said, "and when I squawked that Laurel was my friend, he made a sad face and said she was his friend, too, but he wanted a *woman*."

31

"Husbands," somebody hissed. The fire crackled and flared. Several women looked at their hands as if studying the imprints that marriage and time and maybe too much giving had made. Then they looked up, confused. I recognized that look from years and years of meetings. We were all waiting for someone to make sense of what happened between women and men.

"You know how people embezzle money?" I said. "That's how Jackson embezzled Laurel's life. He pretended it was still in her account, but little by little, he transferred it to his own. And finally, she was bankrupt." I rather liked that. A little flowery, perhaps, and heavy on the metaphor, but not bad. In fact, Alexa Fury could use it to break the gridlock. Mikhail, out in the cold, could take Ariel's hand and say, "Boris has embezzled your happiness."

"Jackson crushed the life out of Laurel," Celia said.

"Then she was too crushable!" Again, it was Janet, the believer. "Women can be party to their own—"

"She was an artist, not a Valkyrie," Celia said.

"And he was a bully!"

"But it's the end of the twentieth century. We're in charge of our own lives!" Janet's strength, or bullheadedness, was awesome. But then, she'd been raised on a different kind of food than the rest of us, nourished by what we'd painfully scraped up from below the surface of our lives.

"Laurel was brainwashed," somebody said.

"Even so, what a pathetic revenge—killing herself to make a point. If he were mine—I'd kill *him!*"

"Not if you were so destroyed you had no more strength," someone reminded her. "That's the whole point."

Nobody had more to add. My turn, then. "Time for a verdict." I ripped paper into twelve slips and each woman searched her purse for pens and pencils.

"I—I abstain," Janet said. She scrambled to her feet and headed for the door. "I won't stop you, but I can't agree. Who made us jury and judge? You're not being fair." And she disappeared into the night.

Fair. I shrugged. Our view of justice was obscured by marital scar tissue, but we did try to be fair.

As fair as Furies can be.

The vote was "guilty." Unanimous—except for Janet's abstention.

"We have our verdict," I said. "What's the sentence?"

"Erin S. Tisiphone, rest in peace," our oldest member said. "And let your betraying bastard of a husband rot where he is."

There were no objections.

So the group now worships Saint Laurel, clever martyr of the war between the sexes.

I consider Laurel's sanctification my most inventive fiction, because, of course, she was not bright or brave enough to frame Jackson.

Laurel lived and died a coward. When Jackson didn't pay support after their separation, she should have dragged him back to court. But she wanted him back, so to avoid harassing him, she decided to sell the netsukes.

I discouraged the idea. I suggested that it wasn't legal to dispose of assets she and Jackson held in common.

In reality, my motives were less about law and more about myself. At the time, I still believed that anything that cost Jackson, cost me.

It didn't matter. As is obvious, she only pretended to listen to me, and she covered her tracks very well with the trip to Chicago and the pseudonym.

I assume that with some invented excuse for the windfall,

she gave her kids the netsuke money while she was alive.

One thing. I am a fair woman, so let's set the record straight. Jackson wasn't a villain. You've heard the evidence. He wasn't much worse than any other man. Certainly better than my poor excuse of a husband had been. Jackson even had moments of decency, like when he gave Laurel his gun. I warned him not to. She was drinking so much by then, she could have blasted anybody who entered the house, including me.

As it turned out, Laurel didn't shoot anybody but herself. But in her own dim way, she managed to do me in, and I resent her for it. After a quarter century of Laurel—and flings with other air heads—Jackson's system couldn't tolerate a strong woman.

So the bastard dumped me for a redheaded, tight-assed, brainless bimbo he flashed all over town. At least we had behaved like adults. We had been discreet. Even after he moved out of his house, we kept a profile lower than a mole's. Not even Laurel suspected. To this day, nobody does.

But what our discretion boils down to is this: Jackson never took me anywhere or bought me so much as a restaurant meal, let alone jewels or anything else of value. I could have used a financial gift or two. I churn out book after book, but it's never enough. I've come to understand that romance doesn't pay.

Anyway, given our secretiveness, I hadn't a clue he was cheating on me until that woman in my book group rushed over to describe, in horrible detail, the passionate scene she'd witnessed between Jackson and the redheaded slut.

And what I really heard her telling me was that I had absolutely nothing left. No Jackson, no husband, no youth, no money, no pride, no hope of anything good ever happening to me again. I hunted Jackson down and we had quite a scene. I humiliated myself, but the man was scum. He kept checking his watch, because his tootsie was waiting.

When you understand how shabbily Jackson treated me, I'm sure you see why he had to be punished, no matter what he did or didn't do to Laurel.

Anyway, that day, after the fight with Jackson, I needed to be with a woman friend, and I figured Laurel understood man troubles. Don't mistake my intent. I wasn't going to say that it was her husband who'd done me wrong. I just figured we could cry in our beers—her beers—together.

Except, midway between our houses, I heard the noise. It wasn't like in the movies or TV. It was massive and definitely final.

I ran to her door and knocked and rang—then I looked through the living room window. Laurel, or what was left of her, was on the couch. There was a gun on the floor, below her dangling hand. She'd taken the coward's way out.

It was awful. Worse than any horror story. I made it back to my place gagging and retching, intending to call emergency, even though I could tell it was all over for Laurel.

And that was when I realized that it didn't have to be all over for me. Why waste the material at hand? With all due modesty, I must say I came up with a concept that was beautiful in its simplicity. But, after all, that is my profession.

Longtime neighbors like we were have each other's house keys. I let myself into Laurel's back door, picked up a chair and bashed in the locked netsuke cabinet. That's when I found out Laurel hadn't listened to me. She'd sold all but six of her netsukes. I nearly cried. My imagined profits had just evaporated, but I reminded myself that money wasn't the main point.

Still, money would have made it sweeter, and lots of money would have made it indescribably delectable, but I had no such luck. In fact, I eventually had to sell my six netsukes cheap in the black market because the murder case made too many headlines for reputable dealers to touch the things. My paltry take in no way compensated for the grief Jackson had caused me. In any case, as a secret netsuke seller myself, you can understand why I nearly had heart failure when Celia decided to play sleuth. Who knows which netsukes and which sales slips she might have unearthed?

Anyway, that evening, I stuffed the tiny carvings in a grocery bag I'd brought because I'd been expecting the full three dozen. Then I lit a cigarette and put it and another lit match on the floor, near where Laurel's hand dangled. When the rug caught, I left by the back door and was in my house in a minute.

And that was that. Except for calling the fire department once I could see flames from my house. And except for my imaginative testimony, which, I can safely say, was my finest hour of storytelling. Besides, I had a willing audience. The cops were young and male. I was middle-aged and female, which is to say, a sexless, unthreatening, powerless and grandmotherly figure in their eyes. They automatically trusted me.

I told them Laurel had told me Jackson was coming over that evening. And I told them Laurel was so pathologically afraid of guns she'd never allow one in the house. And I told them Jackson and Laurel had fought about the netsukes so much that she'd locked them up and hidden the key.

They thanked me for being such a good citizen.

Obviously, it isn't true that all the world loves a lover. The lover's former lover certainly doesn't.

Poor Jackson. He didn't know that. He didn't know anything. He never read the classics and didn't understand what he was saying when he called me a Fury. The fact is, he didn't even understand nonclassical, garden-variety fury.

The kind hell hath none like.

Live and learn.

WHAT'S A WOMAN TO DO?

It was against the rules, eating when you were on duty at the front desk, but he was starving, and who would know, anyway? Nobody else on the force would be back for an hour, and this wasn't the kind of town where citizens burst in, needing to see the police.

Easy for the Chief to say it didn't look good to eat out here. Meanwhile, he was stuffing creamed chicken in his face at the Rotary meeting. Besides, nobody was around for it to look bad to.

Will Pritchett extracted his salami and cheese from the bottom drawer of his desk. Delicious. Extra mayo, too. He took a satisfying bite and read the paper. Guy down in Texas had blown away a dozen people. Will gobbled the news story even more eagerly than the sandwich.

Being a cop in a place like Texas where people get pissed and take out an entire luncheonette would be something, all right. It would be like being a *cop*, not like this job had turned out to be.

He was supposed to be filing, but he looked at the bank of metal cabinets with contempt. He hadn't gone to *clerk* academy. He'd wanted to be a real cop, to curl himself around a doorway, gun at the ready, to handcuff people and read them their rights. Instead, he got stuck with the scut work. Sure, somebody had to do it, like the Chief said, but why him?

The only sounds in the stuffy room were Will's sighs, the wheezing, ancient air conditioner, and the tick of the clock, pushing out one more minute. He shuddered. More like a morgue than a police station. Nothing ever happened here.

She clamped her purse under her right arm and walked resolutely, humming "Feelings," head high despite the wilting heat. Years ago, on a day like today, somebody had actually fried an egg on the sidewalk outside her office. The newspaper came and photographed it. Of course, later on, she'd had to clean up the mess herself. Nobody had any real consideration, even back then.

She felt like that sidewalk egg, edges curling and crisping in the sweltering midday heat. The weather pushed at her nowadays with twice the force it had when she was young. Everything did. She was tired. Of coping. Of trying. Of an entire lifetime of taking care of everything by herself. Had to. Nobody helped anybody. Not even when you were young and reasonably attractive and certainly not when you were a gray-haired old lady.

What was done was done. She could live with what she'd had to do, had been doing, in fact, for a lifetime, but what she couldn't live with was having it all be useless. If people would only be considerate. Leave her in peace. She clutched the navy patent handbag closer, pulled at the flower-sprigged dress where it clung damply to her midriff and directed her canvas shoes toward the police station.

The front door squealed, admitting—of all people—Old Doc Maple, the ogre of his adolescence. A lady dentist was a double humiliation, a combination mother and Nazi torturer, tsking if you hadn't brushed enough for her, poking your mouth with crochet hooks, exhaling the hospital smell of cloves with every breath.

If there was one person in the entire town who would definitely rat to the Chief that he'd been eating a salami sandwich while on duty, it was prissy Missy Doctor Hilda Maple. Will shoved meat, cheese, bread, lettuce and wax paper into the bottom desk drawer, and turned to face his caller.

She stood behind the mahogany banister separating the citizens from the force, lumpy in the kind of dress nobody wore, eyes glinting behind tiny glasses perched on her nose. Standard issue Little Old Lady.

He didn't like her. Who would? Such a prig that at Halloween, she gave out toothbrushes and lectures on dental hygiene. He didn't know if she thought she was giving tricks or treats.

"Help you, Dr. Maple?" Pritchett glanced at the clock. Had to get the filing done, but he wasn't going to let her think he was some kind of clerk. He settled behind his desk.

Hilda Maple pulled a handkerchief with embroidered daisies out of her purse. Her hands looked large and strong, the better to yank the teeth out of your skull. He wondered what Little Old Lady terror had freaked her. Fear of night prowlers? A request for better street lights? A lost pet?

"I've come to confess, Willie," she said.

Sergeant, he wanted to snap. *Will. William. Never* Willie anymore. What did she think, that he was still her little helpless victim? But confess, she'd said. The old biddy was making a joke for probably the first time in her life. He should ease up. He pulled out a chair for her. "What awful thing'd you do, ma'am? Jaywalk? Or—I know—you're really the Texas Terror and you shot all those people at the luncheonette! Hold on while I get those handcuffs."

She frowned and sat down primly, eyeing him like he was a giant tooth and she was going to find a soft spot she could drill into. He wiped all expression off his face and returned her stare until she looked down at her hands. The balance of power had shifted. Doc was old and little Willie Pritchett was a grown-up cop now and this was his turf and his call.

"This is not a joke," she said. "I am here to confess."

"Right." He folded his hands over his middle and waited. He felt a smile tug at his lips.

"The problem is," she said, "my crime was perfect."

Impossible to keep a straight face. She had little pink cheeks, marshmallow fluff hair, a voice like sugar sparkles and tiny feet in white canvas shoes. Not quite a hardened mastermind of the perfect crime. He hid his grin with his hand and stroked his moustache, to look concerned.

"To whom do I confess?" she asked.

"What you see is what you get. Unless you want to wait until Captain and the rest get back. But for now, I am the law." Portis was out sick, the Chief was out lunching and the rest were gone. There'd been a burglary near the shopping center and kids turning on hydrants on Hollyhock Circle, plus, a child on Twentieth was missing—or more likely misplaced, because in this town, there were more hysterical mothers than there were criminals. God, what he wouldn't give for one good solid kidnapping.

"How are you, Willie?" she asked. "As I recall, you had problems with caries and plaque. I hope you're flossing and practicing good maintenance. You don't want gum disease."

She certainly hadn't changed. He glared. His mouth was no longer her damned business. "What really brings you here, ma'am?" he asked.

She stood up again, ramrod straight. He saw moisture marks under her arm, and it pleased him, made up for her posture.

"I do not believe it is improper or excessive for a respectable homeowner to expect a decent night's sleep." She pulled her head back and into her wrinkled neck, like a turtle. She was waiting for him to say something back.

It was like being in school again, breath held, every eye on him as he silently prayed the question, the teacher and the whole classroom would disappear.

"Don't you agree?" She talked like somebody tasting every word before letting go of it.

"Sure." Sure. Whatever she wanted. The old hen was bonkers.

He'd answered right. She smiled, showing good teeth, like a commercial for herself. "You're only given one set," she used to say, clove breath suffocating little Willie, prisoner on her torture chair. "Cherish it."

"With too little sleep, I get shaky," she now said. "A dentist can't have trembling hands. Could drill right through somebody's cheek if you get the shakes."

"You still practicing, then?" Let her know that not only had he stopped being her patient, but he didn't keep track of her. Old biddy should have retired by now, anyway. Age, not insomnia, had given her the shakes.

"I'm trying to practice, but how can I if I can't sleep? My home's impossible now, which is why I want to move to one of your cells. I assume it's quiet here at night, that you enforce the rules, do you not?"

"Whooah. Let me get this straight. You want me to lock you up?" Why did he get all the cranks? Last time it was the guy whose weather stripping talked to him. Now her. "Listen," he said, "is this some kind of— Is Candid Camera out there or something?"

"I believe that constitutionally, as an admitted criminal, I am entitled to a bed here."

Too little sleep and you crack up. He'd seen it in a torture

42

movie. Or was it just age, that old-timer's disease. "Miz Maple, if you're not sleeping good, the doctor could prescribe pills."

"No pill drowns out rock and roll. Nor do earplugs." She bit hard on the edge of every syllable. "They rehearse all night long.

"The Johnson Five." She said it like it was some world-famous group and like she didn't have a clue how funny a name it was.

He couldn't wait to tell the guys. The Johnson Five, they'd told her. Too much. Wonder if one of the Johnsons was named Michael and another Janet, and both their hobbies were having their faces redone.

The old lady closed her eyes for so long, he thought maybe she was catching some of those missed Z's.

He remembered her street. Nice houses. A little past their prime, maybe, but big, on comfortable old-fashioned lots. Much better than he had. "So you're here about this . . . Johnson Five?"

She studied her hands.

"Ma'am?" He half didn't know what to call her. "Doc" had always sounded wrong for a teensy little lady. Kids called her "The Dockess," but that wouldn't do for a professional encounter.

"Hmmm?"

Not only senile, but deaf. The noises she heard started in her head. "You're here because . . ."

"They rehearse in their garage. Back of the property. Every night."

"Then you're here to make a complaint? Disturbing the peace?"

She shook her head. "What's the point? It's Lacey's dog all over again."

43

She was whacko and he was hungry and the air conditioner made the place stink and still be hot and even more than that, damn but he was sick of being a baby-sitter instead of a cop.

"Big, mean, skinny thing, Lacey's dog was." She sounded as if she'd told herself the story exactly the same way, lots of times. It made him queasy, like he was a Peeping Tom or something.

"Some mix of breeds that never should have happened," she continued, stiff-lipped. "Mind you, I *like* dogs. But not that big-headed, long-legged, mud-colored thing."

"Lucky thing it's long gone, then," he said. "You were a good judge of that dog's character, considering what he wound up doing."

"Never shut up. A car, a bird, dandelion fluff went by, it went crazy. I'm not a rich woman and I'm not young anymore. My practice isn't what it was. I couldn't pull up stakes and start over again."

"Lacey's dog is *dead*," he reminded her. His words had no effect. She moved ahead dully, noticing nothing else, like a sleep-walker he'd seen on a movie of the week. He checked the clock. Captain would be back soon and royally pissed if none of the filing was done.

"I tried to befriend it. I *like* animals. But it growled, and squinched its yellow eyes. Couldn't go out and enjoy my garden without it barking and yowling and jumping at the chain link, making it rattle and bang until my head pounded and my hands shook."

"Yes, ma'am, well, now, that sounds real bad, but it's *over*. A dead dog can't bother you. Besides, you came here about something else, am I right?"

"The Johnson Five. Just as bad as that dog ever was. Not sleeping again and afraid just like then that I'll drill right

44

through somebody's cheek, or pull the wrong tooth. Lacey's dog all over again!"

The phone rang, and Will grabbed for it, grateful for a reprieve. Weren't allowed to be rude to them. Didn't dare. Even in a nowhere town like this, people were savvy about police harassment charges. Chief gave pep talks about what he called Gross Insensitivity. "Remember that we are civil *servants*," he always said.

"Sergeant Pritchett speaking," Will said smartly. Old Lady Maple looked impressed. She wasn't the only one with a title, after all. But the caller was only Chuck's wife, asking Will to remind her husband to pick up a cabbage on the way home. Will wrote out the message, hoping Doc couldn't read well upside down. Even the idea of cabbage, a vegetable he didn't like, made his mouth water for the salami and cheese in the bottom drawer. Then suddenly, his heart lurched. God help him—what if the mayo had leaked onto something important! Forms were stacked in that drawer, weren't they? Damn!

"You look startled. Emergency?" she asked after he'd hung up the phone.

"It'll wait." He used his favorite tough, seen-it-all voice. "But not too long," he added as warning. Because his ass would be in a sling if Captain found him wasting his time with an old biddy.

"Did you ever notice her dentures?" Doc asked.

"The dog had false teeth?"

"Lacey did! Terrible clackers. Maybe they gave her a grudge against dentists, or against life. If you can't chew good, you can't live good, is what I always say."

"Ma'am?" He wished he could grab her, shake her a little, get her marbles in place.

"Oh, yes. There'd be a lot less need for head doctors if

more people saw tooth doctors, is what I always say."

"About this problem of yours."

"'He's my watchdog!' Lacey'd screech if I complained, and with every word, her upper plate practically fell out of her mouth. I said her dog could watch plenty good from inside her house. She told me to buy earplugs. Her plates wobbled and clacked. I offered to make a new set for free. Bad teeth, bad chewing, bad digestion, bad temper, is what I say."

"Dr. Maple, Miss Lacey isn't around anymore, and neither is her dog. In all truth, I don't see the point of—"

"That *is* the point. I'm a *nice* person. Nothing worked. Then I called you."

"Me? I've only been on the force a year, ma'am, and Miss Lacey—"

"I mean I filed a complaint with the police. I can prove that part at least. You people keep records, don't you?"

Here it was, then, years later, some kind of lawsuit, like Captain always warned about. Old hen had marched over in her tennis shoes to sue the bejesus out of the department while he was all alone here.

She pulled her little body up even straighter. "You people said there was nothing you could do. Law requires more than one complaint, you said, and I was the only one. Only remove dogs who've attacked somebody, you said."

"Look, the laws are there so people don't make wild accu—"

"The lady who lived on the other side of Lacey was deaf. Still is. Speaks with her hands, you know. The whole row of houses backs onto the big stone retaining wall, so who else is there to hear?" Her voice was less sugar and spice and more like twigs crackling in a fire. "Lacey said that if anything happened to that dog, she'd see that I went to jail. I believed her. You people knew I hated him. Even the deaf woman knew. Isn't that enough proof?"

Proof of what? That she had a complaint against the department? That she was batty? "You know, ma'am Doctor, you said you came about a problem you had *now*." Wanted to be locked up because she couldn't sleep, wasn't that it? He was a trained listener, but this was too much. Her mind wandered all over hell and back. Old Toni Lacey and her dog had been dead and not much missed for a couple years now. "How can we help you?" She was normal enough looking on the outside, but inside, all loose wires. Women went rotten dangerously fast, much quicker than men. This one shouldn't be allowed to handle sharp instruments anymore.

"I don't expect you to help me. Nobody has before. Not once. Always leave me to take care of it on my own. That's why I'm saying this time, give me a quiet cell and a good mattress. I'm too old to do it again."

"Do what? File a complaint?"

She shook her fluff of hair and pursed her mouth. "Take matters in my own hands, you know. Like the other times."

"And which times were they, ma'am?" She looked planted into the floor and likely to stay for days. He smiled to warm her up, then clamped his mouth shut because he wasn't sure the condition of his teeth would pass her inspection. "Ma'am," he said, more loudly than intended, "don't mean to be rude, but hope you don't mind if I work while you talk. Have to take care of some papers." There, that sounded important enough.

He walked to the bank of files and half turned from her as he pulled a stapled set of forms out of the wire basket on top of one cabinet. "Continue," he said. "I'm listening." All ears. Right.

"What happened is this. One day when Lacey went to the

market, I put steak next to the fence. Her stupid animal came right over."

Oh, how he'd dreamed about chasing robbers, finding clues. Being a hero. Not about sweating and filing and enduring a growling stomach while listening to whackos with nobody but him to talk to. Because he was a civil *servant*.

"Soon as his neck was near the chain link, I gave him a shot."

"Wait a minute." He looked over at her. Her purse was under her right arm and her hands were folded in front like a schoolgirl reciting a well-practiced piece. "Who'd you shoot again?"

"The dog."

But Lacey's dog hadn't been shot. Best to simply ignore the woman and get the filing done or the Chief would blame him, like always, even though it wasn't his fault. He looked at the file in his hand. McHooley. Never had gotten it straight if the "Mc" names went before or after the regular "M's."

"When he was out cold," the dentist continued, "I skittled over there into her yard. I must confess, I was rather excited. This was pretty much the professional challenge of my career, you see. I'd prepared a really good mold. Had to work fast, of course, because that stuff hardens like that." She snapped her fingers. "Otherwise, people gag too much. Don't know if you need it that fast for a dog, actually. Don't know if a dog's gag reflex is the same."

He shoved McHooley at the back of the M's while he wondered if he'd really heard the Dockess say she'd put mold on the dog and it hardened and gagged.

"Left him by the fence to sleep off the anesthesia. That was the first quiet afternoon in my garden in a long, long time." She paused and took a deep breath. "Excuse me," she said. "Willie?"

Will turned and faced her directly.

"Shouldn't I be writing this out or dictating it into a machine?"

"Well, ah . . ." What form did they use for hogwash and imaginary confessions? And then, where would he file it? "We'll do that in just a while," Will said. "Meanwhile, I'm trying to get a sense of just what kind of complaint you have." Because I am a *civil* servant.

"But I don't have a complaint! I'm confessing!" Her voice was suddenly shrill.

He rolled his eyes. They'd taught this in training. Lonely people need to feel big, confess crimes they didn't commit. But the cases they talked about at the academy had style. Those people claimed they were serial killers, hijackers, major-league embezzlers. Even the L.O.L.'s imagination was feeble, ending at her garden fence and a moldy dog the Humane Society had put to sleep years ago.

"Sure. Of course," he said. "But all the same, um, why don't we run through your . . . confession . . . once. Kind of a . . . rehearsal. So it's fresh and clear in your mind. It's standard procedure."

"And that is exactly what's wrong with this country today! Bureaucratic rules and routines! Inefficiency! Duplication, everything in triplicate. But all right, then. The dog slept it off most of the afternoon, but he was back to himself by dark, and he barked all night long."

Will tsked sympathetically. Anybody still complaining about being kept up by a long-dead dog needed handling with kid gloves.

"However," she said with her schoolmarm enunciation, "that particular night, I didn't mind his barking because I didn't intend to sleep, anyway. I worked straight through in my lab. Years before, I had learned to run in essence my own laboratory. I had a run-in with a lab man because I was female. Sexual harassment didn't start with the young women of today."

Exactly what he wanted, a noontime lecture on women's rights.

"But," she said, "the lab man was long ago, in a different city and there's no point in discussing him."

Maybe, just to shake her up, shut her up, he should do what she wanted: book her and throw her in a cell. But the Chief would kill him. He could just see the headlines about police brutality with a photo of Hilda Maple behind bars, her white hair like fake Christmas snow.

"The point of the lab man, however," she said, "is that way back when, I learned to do my own lab work, and to do it perfectly. I'm a perfectionist, you see. That night in particular, my work was superb. I wished I could have shown them off. In fact, today, the thought struck me that when I'm incarcerated, I might write it up for a professional journal."

Lady, lady, you need a shrink and I need food. He wondered if he should call an ambulance, have her institutionalized for her own good and the safety of all the little victims she still tortured.

"The next day, I went over," the light little voice continued. "Lacey was making tea. She told me to get out, threatened to pour boiling water on me. I tried reasoning with her. I *like* people. I'm a *good* neighbor. But she was impossible, so I just plain grabbed her and stuck in the needle. Same stuff I gave the dog. First, she opened up to scream. I tell you, the sight of those ill-fitting, shoddy false teeth of hers made *me* want to scream. Her eyes got fluttery and closed, and I clamped those doggie dentures onto her neck and let them bite down, hard. Very hard."

"Dentures? False teeth for dogs?"

"Well, not *for* the dog, really. But if dogs wore them, these would have been the best. I am a perfectionist."

"Now listen, ma'am—"

"I know what you're about to say. There's more to it than a bite mark. Forensic science, am I right?"

He had no idea what she was talking about. Besides, Nichols had misspelled a name again. Was anybody really named Shcwartz? He'd file it the way it said, and then guess who would get in trouble when the file couldn't be found?

"I know you people check things out, so I'd collected some of the dog's saliva, too, when I took the impression. Your labs would question the authenticity of the bite, otherwise."

She looked so earnest. So sincere. Was it maybe possible that she had really made a set of dog teeth and bitten old Lacey to death?

"If you check your files there, you'll see that everything I'm telling you is accurate," she said mildly.

She melted back into Mrs. Santa with her halo of cotton batting. God! She'd had him going for a second. Of course her story would mesh with the files. She'd had years to work on it. It meant nothing. Nothing meant anything except his getting the filing done. He was in enough trouble with the Chief already without dragging the Case of the Crazy Lady Dentist in front of him, creating more work for everybody and more filing for himself.

"When she was quite dead, I took her teapot." Doc Maple's voice was eager and precise. "The one she was going to throw on me. I poured some of the steaming water on the floor, then I opened the door. The monstrous dog started at me, but I had steak ready again and as soon as he took it, I shot the needle in him, too, and he went ga-ga. I poured the rest of the boiling water on his paw. I was sorry about that, but it was necessary. It must have stung when he woke up.

51

Then I dropped the kettle on the floor and put the pot holder next to it."

Two years since old lady Lacey died. Maybe living next door to all the hullabaloo at the time had given Doc Maple a—what was it? He'd just read about it—a trauma. Maybe she was in post-traumatic shock. He sighed and turned around.

"And you know the rest of the story," she said.

Everybody did. It was ancient history. Lacey and her dog were long since buried next to each other, like Lacey had requested in her will. There'd been a lot of flak about that, you can bet. Even an editorial in the paper. After all, Miss Lacey had made that request before her dog turned. But people said to leave it for pet and master heaven, where the dog could forgive Lacey for pouring boiling water on his paw and Lacey could forgive him for reacting with his teeth on—or in, really—her neck.

"Yes, indeed, I know that story," Will said standing straight, sucking in his gut and allowing himself a slight professional scowl. Enough was enough.

"But what I said was *true!*"

"Of course it was." He went back to his desk, worry gnawing at him as much as hunger did. He gently opened the bottom desk drawer and saw his worst fears confirmed. Leaking mayonnaise had made the Form 15-A's transparent. Damn. How would he explain this one? He closed the drawer and turned back to her. "Look, ma'am," he said briskly, "we need some proof, some evidence of your, ah, alleged crime."

She shook her head. "I destroyed everything when it happened. I had no idea I'd ever want to be caught."

"Well, then." His stomach growled.

"You won't give me a cell?"

"Oh, Doc Maple, come on. They're for criminals."

She turned and walked away.

52

"But you came here about that band!" he called after her. "Didn't you want to file a complaint?"

"What's the use? It still takes two complaints and the deaf woman is still there on the other side and the wall is still in the back. All my life I've known that if I wanted something done, I'd have to do it myself. I was hoping this one time would be different." She sighed. "Never mind, then." She pushed the door open and was gone.

Imagine that. He stared at the door as if her afterimage were still on it. Hallucinating that she'd killed somebody with false teeth. Once a dentist, always a dentist. Wait till he told the guys. But what would he do with those greasy forms?

She should have known better. Did she think that knights still roamed the land looking to save damsels in distress? Even if they did, men in armor didn't rush to the aid of gray-haired damsels. Nobody did. She'd have to do it herself. Again.

She didn't count the ones when she was really young, or even the dorm roommate and that god-awful woman in the apartment next to hers, the one who screamed all the time. You couldn't blame the police for not helping with those problems because she hadn't even asked them to. She was pretty cocky about taking care of everything herself back in those days.

As for the lab man, who could she have asked for help? There weren't even laws against that sort of thing back then, the dirty things he said, the way he "accidentally on purpose" bumped and rubbed against her. A woman was on her own in those days. It still made her smile to have poisoned him with a dentifrice. Sodium perborate, and how appropriate. A cleaning agent to permanently clean—and close—a filthy mouth.

After the roommate and the screamer and the lab man,

she'd rented a house in a new neighborhood and expected peace and quiet, but she never got her wishes, no matter how simple they were. Because in that house, there'd been Charlie Mallory next door with his so-called antique car collection. Hammering, battering, and gunning of motors! She'd gone to the police that time, but they were as dim and insensitive a group as they were here, so she took care of it. Charlie was gone all day long, so tinkering with his precious car wasn't much of a problem. She knew physics and chemistry. Dentists had scientific minds, after all.

The explosion left a mess, though. They buried what was left of Charlie, and that should have been that, but car debris was all over, even in her backyard. Then the landlord, who owned both houses, raised her rent for repairs. Wasn't fair and she didn't like the bombed-out look next door, so she'd moved here, where she was positive things would be better. And they were, for a long while. Except then, bad luck again when Lacey got her dog.

It would have been nice if the police hadn't left it to her to take care of the Lacey problem, but on the other hand, she'd had the chance to rise to the challenge and be creative. The dentures were much more inventive than the poisons and the bomb had been.

She sighed. Maybe she'd peaked with those false teeth. Certainly didn't have as good an idea about the Johnson Five. There was that pool they'd dug—and what a racket the workers had made! A swimming accident, perhaps, while drugged? Everybody knew about teenagers, especially the musical ones. Laughing gas, maybe?

Why did people keep doing this to her? Keep creating these situations?

The drummer first. Definitely the worst of them.

Or maybe electrocution in the pool? They kept speakers

and guitars with wires and all manner of things too close to the water.

It was possible that they'd replace the drummer, that the rest of them would have to go, too.

Perhaps a car accident? A few of them all at once, that way, and heaven knew they drove too fast, that kind, so maybe . . .

But even after she took care of all five Johnsons, there'd still be more to do. She was sick and tired of the police's insensitivity. Patronizing her that way, that stupid Willie with the film on his teeth!

What good were laws if they didn't apply to the important things? And who needed police if they didn't enforce anything? She'd be doing a public service, getting rid of them, easing the tax rolls.

Willie had always been obnoxious, even as a child. He'd be a good place to start—right after the Johnsons.

Little Willie Pritchett shouldn't be much of a problem. She remembered how he'd come into her office years ago, bits of food still lodged between his teeth. Always eating, that one. And even today, she'd seen him shove a sandwich in the desk drawer, seen the glob of mayonnaise caught on his poorly shaved chin. A piggy man. So food it would be. At work. Something he could sneak. Something quick . . .

She walked carefully, brow slightly wrinkled, a little old lady in a flowered dress and tennis shoes, humming "Feelings." Nobody noticed her.

ONE BEAUTIFUL BODY

English teachers do not have power lunches.

It took a while to get this concept across to Ivy Jean Hoffman, but then, we moved in different circles.

I was surprised to find Ivy Jean still in Philadelphia. I had thought she'd moved on as literally as she had figuratively. I was still more surprised to find her in my neighborhood, and I was stupefied to find her in a supermarket, since she and food have been at war longer than the Arabs and the Israelis. Then I noticed that her cart contained nothing to chew or slurp or gnaw. It was piled high with non-edibles. A dozen boxes of designer facial tissues, an industrial-sized aluminum foil, bundles of soap, three colors of toilet paper, and five boxes of plastic wrap. I wondered what leftovers she wrapped in the plastic and foil.

"Amanda Pepper!" she chirped. "I don't believe it!" Which gives you an idea of her sincerity. She knew my center-city address and she also knew that unlike her, I ate, so why shouldn't she believe I'd forage for food in my own neighborhood?

We sent make-believe kisses across our carts. Ivy's face barely moved. Way back when we were both eleven years old, she mastered the starlet's wide-eyed amazed stare to avoid building future wrinkles.

"I live right across the square now," she said.

I was not going to join Welcome Wagon.

"Finished redoing our condo this morning."

Maybe that's what she'd encase in plastic wrap.

"You have to see it. Must be time for our annual lunch, anyway." She pulled an organizer out of an alligator bag and flipped pages, looking for a window of opportunity in which to fit me. "Oh, dear," she murmured, "no wonder I'm stressed out."

I explained why I, too, would have difficulty making a date. With five sections of English, one study hall, one year-book meeting, and sporadic lunch duty, I didn't "lunch." Furthermore, my school's definition of an hour was as skimpy as a psychiatrist's, though less well paid.

Ivy Jean Hoffman responded to the facts of my life with incredulity. "I can't believe you stand for being treated like a *slave!*" Her outrage made it clear, as it was intended to, that she was treated and paid extremely well and I was a mere lackey. "But we *have* to get together," she wailed. "Isn't there any time at all?"

We both knew weeks had more than five days, but we also knew that Saturday and Sunday were for fun, not for each other. "I have a free period after lunch Thursdays," I said. If I didn't prepare lesson plans or meet with disgruntled students, I could extract an hour and a half midday.

"But Thursday's perfect! This coming one I'm having the reunion committee to lunch. Nikki and I are co-chairs." Nikki was another high-school acquaintance and Ivy's business partner. "You zip over, you hear?" Sometimes Ivy played Southern Belle, although the high school she was re-uniting had been just slightly west of Philadelphia.

"I really don't want to be on the reunion committee," I said.

"I hear you. Come anyway, Mandy. It'll be fun!"

I doubted that. Ivy Jean was a legacy. Our mothers had been close friends and so desperately wanted us to follow suit that the fact that we disliked each other from conception on didn't matter. Year after year, Ivy and I shared celebrations: we sat next to each other at *The Nutcracker* each December at the Academy of Music; we watched our dads burn burgers on July Fourth; we rode the waves at Beach Haven and even shared a high-school graduation party.

And still and all, Ivy—to me—was selfish, shallow, and stupid, and I was—to her—bookish, unstylish, and boring.

But when we were finally, happily separated in college, Ivy's mother died in a terrible automobile crash. Embarrassingly soon after, her father married a creature who kept forgetting there was such a person as Ivy and, somehow, Ivy's father's memory also failed. Ivy's bed was donated to Goodwill and the room quickly filled with cribs for newborn twin boys. That's about when Ivy began using me as a touchstone, proof that she did, indeed, exist.

She was obnoxious, self-obsessed, and unreliable, but she was also truly unmoored and lost. She gave a new meaning to the word insecure. It seemed little enough to shore her up, give her a personal history fix, prove that somebody remembered her. I was her past. And that is why, once a year, two women who didn't like each other nonetheless "did" lunch. Our table talk was always the same. First, we validated the past with a round of nostalgia in which celebrations remembered were infinitely more pleasurable than they'd been when actually lived. Then we validated her present. We did Ivy—Ivy's face, Ivy's body, Ivy's food, Ivy's problems, Ivy's business, and Ivy's husband, all of which topics were basically interchangeable.

Ivy had been an unpopular child. She was convinced this had been due to her having been plain and pudgy.

I thought her obsessive concern with her appearance would subside once she snared Mitchell and married him, but I'd been wrong. Their marriage wasn't the answer to anything. Body size was. Ivy knew the caloric count of every menu listing in North America and the details of every get-thin-quick scam. I have "lunched" with her when she ate only red meat, only bananas, only protein, only carbohydrates, only beans and rice, only fruit, only fruit juice, only water. I listened to details of spas visited, diet gurus consulted, wraps and massages attempted, and lips suctioned.

I listened and nodded. Now and then I said she would kill herself dieting. "You'll be a beautiful corpse," I'd say. An old joke, but she never laughed.

In the gospel according to Ivy Jean, goodness equaled thinness. Virtue equaled trimness, success equaled freedom from cellulite. Her single measure of man—or woman—was the span of the waist, hips, and thighs. Evil was "letting yourself go."

Five years ago, Ivy Jean turned her private obsession into public cash. She co-created "The You Within," or TYW to the initiated, a high-priced diet boutique that promised not only to unveil the thin woman smothered inside your flab, but to outfit her, style her hair, and set her free.

A ripe and timely idea. Ivy and Nikki now had three clinics and a fourth due to open. There was talk of nationwide franchising.

I bent over my grocery cart and camouflaged my half gallon of ice cream with a low-cal TV dinner. "Sounds like things are going wonderfully for you."

She rolled her eyes. Eyeballs never wrinkled, so she was fairly free with hers. "There's a reason I stock up on aspirin." And indeed, an economy-size bottle of extra-strength headache pills contained the only ingestible items in her basket.

"Just between us," she said, "I haven't been too brilliant about picking partners. I'm talking business and marriage."

I knew her anxiety was sincere because she scowled, activating muscles and risking lines. "I wouldn't tell anybody but you," she continued, "because you're practically family, but Nikki makes me so *nervous* the way she fights over every penny the business needs—and I *eat* when I'm nervous and I'm becoming a *house*—and what will that do to my *business?* Nothing *fits* and I have a TV spot for TYW to shoot next week! An *ad!* She's *destroying* me, and if she—" She stopped herself, looking momentarily confused. Once off the topic of herself, she was on unsteady ground. "And you?" she finally said with an air of discovery. "What's new?"

"Nothing much. Still teaching."

"And men?"

"Kind of." I didn't think she could understand the allure of my now and then, mostly now, thing with a homicide cop like C.K. Mackenzie. After all, it was my opinion that Ivy's husband Mitchell could be replaced by a boa constrictor—as long as the snake was rich—and nobody, most of all Ivy, would notice.

There was talk that Ivy Jean craved husbands—anybody's—the way other women lusted for chocolate. She had even once computed how many calories were burned at an assignation.

"Hmmm," Ivy said, spotting the Rocky Road in my cart. "Ice cream. Sixty percent fat. You know my saying: a minute on the lips, a lifetime on the hips." She seemed much cheerier, buoyed like a missionary who'd stumbled across a native worshiping tree roots. "I have a wonderful chart of fat percentages I want to share with you on Thursday," she said. "And don't worry. Lunch will be simple. I'll make something light."

★ ★ ★ ★ ★

The elevator deposited me in the foyer of Ivy's condo. The others were already there—partner Nikki and five other former classmates, all contemplating Ivy's locked door. We rang, knocked, chitted and chatted, but by twelve-fifteen, I was hungry and edgy.

"She does this all the time," Nikki grumbled. "Most unreliable—"

"I'm going downstairs," I said. "The lobby has chairs. And a phone. I'll call her. Maybe she fell asleep. Anybody want to join me?"

We all packed into the small elevator and descended. The lobby was not much larger than Ivy's foyer and it had a total of three chairs. We became excessively polite and democratic, which meant that none of us used the chairs. We all stood in a clump near a woman in a glow-in-the-dark lime outfit. She guarded a large carton filled with Styrofoam containers. "Mrs. Hoffman expected me half an hour ago," she whispered harshly at the guard. "I'm her *caterer*."

"But ma'am, I buzzed her apartment. She isn't home." He wore a cranberry uniform trimmed smartly in gold braid, but he looked defeated, as if he'd been drummed out of the corps but allowed to keep the costume.

"You don't understand! She wanted me out before her—she's expecting—" She finally noticed us, did a quick count, added one for the missing hostess, and her shoulders sagged. She lowered her voice, but we could all still hear her. "She didn't want her guests to know I'm doing the—"

So the simple and light thing Ivy made was a telephone call. It didn't really surprise me. Ivy was afraid of touching food, as if calories could be absorbed through the fingertips.

"Couldn't I set up and leave?" The caterer was frantic.

61

"Now my next order's late, too. I'm going to lose every client I have! *Please?*"

The guard considered her, her carton, and the unscary seven of us. "Well," he said, "she did tell me about this little party of hers. I have the guest list, so if I could double-check your names, ladies, I don't see why I couldn't let you into Mrs. Hoffman's." Slowly, slowly, demanding driver's licenses and a major credit card for I.D., he went through the list.

While the first of our group went through the guard's routine, Nikki seemed to lose it, but quietly. "Damn Ivy. Completely inconsiderate and self-centered. She probably forgot. Found something more exciting, like aerobics in bed. A nooner. With whoever."

"Whomever," I murmured.

"You shouldn't say that, Nikki!" For a second, I thought I had an ally, but Barby White wasn't talking grammar. I could see her eyes moisten.

"Sorry!" Nikki snapped. "I didn't say *who,* did I?"

Whom, I said, but silently.

Barby White sniffed.

"Well, then," Nikki said, "if the shoe fits, wear it."

Bad grammar and excessive use of clichés. It was obvious that Nikki was no good.

"You're so mean!" Barby wailed.

"Come on," Nikki said. "Grow up. Sometimes the truth hurts, but knowledge is power. You'll get over it and so will he. He'll come back. Ivy has a short attention span."

The guard called Nikki's name.

Barby stood to my right, by herself. Her skin flushed, then drained, pale to beet-borscht red to pasty bloodlessness.

I was almost as stunned as she. Zoological images filled my brain. Nikki was a snake, a cat, a cur, a rat. The rest of the reunion committee seemed to agree. I heard a whispered chorus of reactions on my left.

"That was way, way below the belt."

"But Barby must have known, don't you think? I mean if *we* did, surely she must!"

"It was obvious that she knew. Why else would she react that way? But all the same . . ."

"I don't think she did. The wife's always last. Besides, would Barby be on Ivy's committee if she knew?"

The guard decided that Nikki was who she was and called Barby. Looking loose and flabby, like one who had definitely Let Herself Go, Barby turned to nobody in particular and said, "My husband wouldn't sleep with that broomstick." But she walked to the guard like someone drugged.

"Neither will Ivy's husband," somebody said. "His girlfriends tend to be voluptuous."

One by one we were okayed by the guard and then finally admitted into the absolute splendor of Ivy Jean Hoffman's abode. Muted, exquisite colors were on the glazed walls, oversized paintings, bleached and waxed floors, rich fabrics, fresh flowers in exquisite vases. It was, in short, your generic incredibly rich person's living room.

We whispered, as if in a museum, running reverent light hands over smooth woods and exquisite accessories, and then we sank into downy sofas and waited.

And waited some more. Half my break time and all my patience were now completely gone. "I'm going to have to leave," I said.

"Me, too," another woman said. "Do you think I could take a peek around before I go?"

"Might as well while you can," Nikki said. Her mood seemed permanently soured ever since the altercation with Barby. "The creditors will probably be up to repossess it before the next reunion committee meeting."

She greeted our shocked expressions with a shrug. "It's no big secret. Ivy's uncontrolled spending on this place has Mitchell near bankruptcy. He's always saying so."

"He must be using hyperbole," I suggested.

"I don't know who he's using," Nikki said. "But I know he probably couldn't afford anybody too expensive anymore."

"Exaggerating," I said. "Using a figure of speech."

Nikki raised an eyebrow. "I know Ivy and her spending, so I doubt that he's hyper anything."

Maybe because our curiosity was the only thing we could feed, we began investigating, heading for the kitchen first, perhaps hoping for a stray grape or cracker. Instead, we found a twenty-first-century laboratory, a prototype for a space station, with not an alien microbe in sight. Except for what the harried caterer had forgotten to remove. A Styrofoam container and two salad dressing lids lay on the black granite counter. I personally thought plastic pollutants were a wonderful touch, and very much in keeping with the futuristic theme, but somebody joked about how angry Ivy would be. On behalf of the caterer's future, I tidied up. It took a while to find the compactor and when I did, it was filled to the brim with more Styrofoam boxes floating atop a sea of plastic wrap, but I shoved my trash in, slammed the gizmo shut, and pushed the button to squeeze it all in. Ivy's kitchen was now the way she liked things—devoid of any sign of life.

We moved on, stomachs growling in the lettuce-colored dining room where the bread sticks and salads the caterer had put out looked as good as the baronial decor. We toured Mitchell's paneled lair, admiring its "manly" color scheme and aroma, both dark, both tobacco, and the ornately carved racks—one for pipes, the other displaying antique, expensive pistols. We moved to the media center, electronics swaddled in fine cabinetry that silently opened at the push of a hidden control panel. We murmured through Ivy Jean's Art Deco home office, and in the mirrored state-of-the-art gymnasium we stared at our non-state-of-the-art reflections.

And then we reached the master bedroom.

Nikki had been right. Ivy Jean was in bed. But she'd been wrong about the rest. Ivy was alone and she wasn't doing aerobics because she wasn't doing breathing. There was a large and ugly hole in the center of her chest and an ivory-handled gun in her hand on the bloodstained spread.

I don't know who screamed first, but the whole group backed up. Some, gagging, rushed off to bathrooms. Barby, skin now parchment hue, shook her head, over and over, and Nikki exhaled loudly, the way you do when a hard job is finished.

I stared, horrified and immeasurably sad for Ivy and the dead body she'd never enjoyed. I looked at the wisp on the bed, all bones and no conviction, a heartbreaking waste, and wished for another chance at lunch with her, another chance to convince her that she did, indeed, exist.

"Don't touch anything," I whispered to whichever committee members were still in the room. It was a foolish thing to utter, even in a whisper, because we'd already fondled and stroked most of the apartment. "I'll call the police," I added. At least that made sense.

A gaggle of specialists appeared. Some headed for the bedroom to inspect, identify, and label, and others questioned the reunion committee.

"Why on earth are you keeping us?" I asked Mackenzie. I was being interrogated in a flowery, wickery guest bedroom. "I have to leave or my tenth graders will never know 'The Rime of the Ancient Mariner.'"

"Movin' fast as we can," he said. Whatever our relationship, when push comes to shove, what matters is that he's a cop. Especially at a crime scene. I was given permission to use the guest room telephone to call my school. The brief and painful conversation that ensued gave me a brain ache. My principal has remarkably low tolerance for staff involvements in unnatural deaths.

"An entire classroom of kids who'll never thrill to 'Water, water everywhere, and not a drop to drink.' And now I'm in big trouble, too."

"I'll write you an excuse," Mackenzie said. "Now, tell me everythin' about Ivy Jean Hoffman."

I did just that, back to communal *Nutcracker* outings and forwards through today's gossip. "And that's it. And none of it explains why she'd kill herself," I concluded.

"She didn't."

"But—the gun, I saw, we all saw—"

"Somebody wanted you to think she did. For starters, she shouldn't have been holdin' it. Gun shoots out of the hand of a real suicide. And if she'd fired it, powder burns would be on the front and back of her hand, not just the palm, like they are. There's even somethin' peculiar, somethin' wrong about the bullet hole itself . . ."

"Murdered," I said. "Murdered. But why whom?"

"From what you said, there was enough money and sex and cheatin' and anger right in the committee for a whole passel of murders."

"That was only talk. Besides, none of us was in here until after she was dead."

He lifted an eyebrow. "How 'bout somebody comin' up earlier? Ivy'd let any one of you in and then, bang, she'd be dead and you could leave. Later, you come back and look innocent. That's why we're checkin' y'all for powder burns."

"That's ridiculous. How do you think we arranged for her to undress, lie down, and be shot?"

Mackenzie paced the small room. "I need to work on that part."

"Furthermore, the front door was locked."

"Door locks automatically when you close it."

"The guard," I said. "He knows who came up here."

"This one's shift started at noon and he says the mornin' guy's the building owner's nephew. He flunked out of drug rehab and tends to sleep on the job when he isn't drinkin'. Didn't log a single visitor to the building all mornin', let alone the last hour. Frankly, I think the tenants could save a lot of money by replacin' him with a photo of a guard. Be just as effective."

"Why'd you single out the last hour as important for visitors?" I asked.

"That's when she was killed. Her temperature's still normal, so figure it out yourself. A body drops a degree and a half an hour, more or less. And a skinny thing like her with no body fat would cool down fast. No insulation."

"She thought she was fat," I murmured.

"Rigor's movin' fast, but she's pretty muscular," he said. "A weird thing—the body's salty. Must've worked out and not showered. Lay down for a nap, maybe?"

"Sweaty? On her brand-new spread?" But before I could further explain domestic niceties, there was an explosion of male sounds outside. Mitchell Hoffman was back in his castle. We went out to watch.

"Why would Ivy do such a terrible thing?" he wailed. "Why?" He put his hand to his face as if hoping there were tears there. There were not. He dropped his hand. He was a rotten actor and obviously had no idea of how grief felt.

After he'd been taken aside and informed that it was

murder, he erupted. "Where's goddamned security? What are we paying for? I'll have their heads, by God, I'll—"

No horror, no sorrow, no tears, no surprise, no questions, especially the ones about who would do such a terrible thing or why anyone would consider it. My money was on Mitchell, and after Mackenzie had finished questioning him, I said so.

The detective sighed. "He has motive, sure. In over his head and couldn't afford a divorce. It's his gun, too. But he also has an alibi. He's been, since nine a.m., in a corporate strategy meeting—don't ask what that means—and he has one dozen witnesses for every minute of it. Includin' trips to the men's room, he says. So. Cherchez la femme. Or les femmes, perhaps?"

Aiding and abetting Mackenzie's suspicions, neither Nikki nor Barby had decent alibis. Nikki claimed to have worked alone at home all morning and Barby had been in and out of stores, killing time, not Ivy. Unfortunately, she'd bought nothing and no salesperson was likely to remember her.

They found no powder burns on any of us, but we'd had lots of time to wash or chemically treat our hands or do whatever killers did to hide evidence.

"Why aren't you thinking about a lover?" I demanded. Mackenzie and I had relocated to a corner of the living room, where we were eyed suspiciously by my former high-school classmates, as if we were forming a clique and snobbishly excluding them. "Somebody with a key who didn't even talk to the guard," I said. "Because if it wasn't a lover, why was she lying naked on top of the bedspread?"

"No signs of sex so far. Could she have sweat enough in anticipation to make herself salty? Or maybe the caterer . . ." Mackenzie mused. "Maybe she was already up here first and—"

"If you'd seen the woman, heard her, you'd know how far-fetched that is. She called Ivy 'Mrs. Hoffman' and she was scared to death of losing her as a customer." Mention of the caterer triggered thoughts of all her work, of the wilting salads. "That food's going to spoil." I couldn't even repackage it, since I'd crushed all the containers in that gizmo. "Should I wrap and refrigerate it?" I asked, hoping to snag a lettuce leaf. I was exceedingly hungry, even though it was probably inappropriate to feel such mundane urges at this time. "You don't need it as evidence. She wasn't poisoned, after all."

"Don't touch anything, okay?" Mackenzie said.

Something nagged at me besides hunger. Something I'd already said echoed, but too distantly to catch.

"She really thought she was fat?" Mackenzie asked.

I nodded. "Obsessed. You've seen her at her worst, though. With clothes on, she didn't look that scrawny." It was a shame she'd died naked. As soon as they allowed, I'd dress her as a last act of decency.

More mental nagging. Bits and pieces of the day bumped and clumped in my mind, like magnetic shavings. I sifted through them. Ivy. Ivy, of course. The Ancient Mariner. Water, water. Obsession. Sex. Salt. The incompetent guard. Salty bedspread. Mitchell and money. Perfection. Mitchell and other women. Ivy and other men. Quick rigor mortis. Water, water.

Now I was not only hungry, but thirsty. I wondered if I could disturb the scene of the crime, or at least the water faucet. I'd wear gloves and leave no fingerprints. But even so, a human touching anything in that pristine house was an intrusion. Ivy appeared to have been as fanatical about her house as she'd been about her body.

Pathetic Ivy. So driven and frightened and needy. So *hungry*.

69

Anorexic Ivy complaining last Friday that she was too fat, that a TV commercial for TYW would be ruined.

Ivy shopping for nonfood. Five boxes of plastic wrap and not a leftover to cling to.

The compactor. Styrofoam floating on a sea of—"Mackenzie," I said. "I have it."

"I've known that for a while now."

"I'm talking about Ivy's murder."

He raised an eyebrow.

"Could body temperature be a wrong estimate of time of death?"

He shrugged. "Sure, if, say, the victim had a fever when she died and the coroner didn't know it, or if the temperature of the room was real high or low. Things like that."

"Or a thing like the corpse had been done up like a mummy in plastic wrap?"

"What's that? A kinky sex trick?"

"A kinky diet trick. To sweat off pounds. Instant sauna."

"You're kidding."

"Dangerous. It can raise your core temperature." I'd read that warning in a fitness magazine. I read about diet and exercise a lot, trusting my muscles to acknowledge my good intentions and firm and tone themselves.

"Well, well, well," he drawled. "Her core temperature was up and she was sweating. The Case of the Salty Corpse. Amanda Pepper does it again."

"Yards of plastic wrap in the compactor," I said. "I assumed the caterer put it there, but she used Styrofoam containers. Ivy put it there."

"Correction: Amanda Pepper almost does it again. Ivy's murderer put the plastic wrap in there. She was shot while she was wrapped. Pretty much point-blank, but it wouldn't seem logical to imply that a woman had wrapped herself in plastic before shooting herself, would it? That's why the wound looked odd. I'll bet the lab finds melted or fused plastic wrap in it, but even so, they'd never have guessed why."

"So you think the killer saw that she was wrapped up and fairly immobile—certainly couldn't jump up and trot away easily—shot her and unwrapped her—"

"And put the gun in her hand," Mackenzie added, "and—"

"—left for a corporate strategy session." We smiled at each other. For once, the most logical suspect was the most logical suspect. "And sober, stoned or not, the guard didn't log anybody coming up here because nobody did. The mister left for work, that's all."

"So maybe," Mackenzie said slowly, "instead of givin' you a note for your principal, we should give you a police citation."

"I'd settle for a late lunch."

"How do cheeseburgers with fries sound?"

"Here? In this house? Pornographic. Sacrilegious. Depraved. But I want onion rings, too. And Rocky Road and Oreos afterward." I would exorcize the diet devil who had possessed Ivy Jean until only bones, obsession, and plastic wrap were left.

Poor lost Ivy. Rest in peace.

I hoped she could, but I doubted it. What, after all, would she do for all eternity with no body of her own or others to criticize and desperately try to improve?

In order to tackle such a metaphysical puzzler, my brain required feeding. And so began my first annual Ivy Jean Hoffman Memorial Lunch.

In the end, out of respect, I told them to hold the onion rings.

GOODBYE, SUE ELLEN

"I don't want a lifetime supply of chewing gum! I want *stock!*" Ellsworth Hummer looked around the conference table, pausing to glare at each of the other directors of Chatworth Chewing Gum, Incorporated.

Neither Peter Chatworth (Shipping), Jeffrey Chatworth (Advertising), Oliver Chatworth (Product Control), Agatha Chatworth (Accounting), nor Henry Chatworth (Human Resources) glared back. Instead, each adopted a rather sorrowful expression. Then they turned their collective attention to the chairperson of the board, Sue Ellen Chatworth Hummer.

Sue Ellen looked at her red-faced husband. "We've told you before, honey," she said in her sweetest voice, "Daddy didn't want it that way. This is the Chatworth *family* business."

"I'm family now, aren't I?"

His response was a mildly surprised widening of six pairs of disgustingly similar Chatworth eyes.

"You're my *husband* now, honey, but you're a Hummer, not a Chatworth," Sue Ellen said, purring. "Besides, you should be happy. After all, you're president of the company."

Ellsworth Hummer's blood percolated. She made it sound like playing house—you be the mommy and I'll be the daddy. Only Sue Ellen's game was, You play the president and I'll be the chairperson for real. His title was meaningless as long as Sue Ellen held the stock in her name only.

He'd received the position as an extra wedding gift from his bride, six months earlier, but all it had yielded so far was a lot of free chewing gum. And now, for the sixth time in as many months, the board had voted him down, denied him any real control, any stock, any say.

Ellsworth stood up. The chair he'd been on toppled backwards and landed with a soft thunk on the thick Persian carpet. "I'm sick of Daddy and his rules!" he shouted. "Sick of Chatworths, one and all! Sick of chewing gum!"

"You can't truly mean that." Cousin Peter sounded horrified.

"I do!" Ellsworth shouted.

"But honey," Sue Ellen said, "chewing gum has kept the Chatworths alive. Chewing gum is our life! How can you possibly be sick of it?"

"What's more," Ellsworth said, "I am not interested in anything else you have to say, or in any of the business on the agenda today or in the future." And he left, slamming the heavy door behind him, cursing the fate that had brought him so far, and yet not far enough.

Once home, he settled into the lushly paneled room Sue Ellen had redecorated for him. She called it his "study" although she'd been unable to tell him what important documents he was supposed to study in there, so he used the room to study the effects of alcohol on the human nervous system. It was the most hospitable room in the rambling, semi-decrepit mansion Sue Ellen had inherited. The place had gone to seed after Mrs. Chatworth's death and Sue Ellen had been too busy being his bride—she said—to begin renovations yet. So Ellsworth spent a great deal of time in his study. Now he poured himself a brandy and considered his options.

Sue Ellen owned the house. Sue Ellen owned the company. And Sue Ellen owned him. That was not at all the way things were supposed to have worked out.

Divorce was not an option. He had signed a prenuptial agreement because, long ago, Sue Ellen's daddy had reminded her that she'd better not forget that husbands were outsiders, not family. All a split would get him was a one-way ticket back to his mother's shack, or, God help us all, to a nine-to-five job. Ellsworth shuddered at the thought of either possibility.

There was only one logical solution. Aside from what she made as chairperson of the present-day company, Sue Ellen was rich in trust funds and the fruits of earlier chewing gum sales, and he was Sue Ellen's legal heir. Ergo, Sue Ellen had to die.

He sighed, not with distaste for the idea itself, but for the work and effort involved in it. This was not how he'd envisioned the happily-ever-after part. He sighed again, and squared his shoulders. He was equal to the task and would do whatever was necessary to achieve his destiny.

All he'd been gifted with at birth was a well-designed set of features and a great deal of faith in himself. His mother, poor in every other way, was rich in hope. Her favorite phrase had always been, "You'll go far, Ellsworth."

And as soon as it was possible, he had.

He'd kept on going, farther and farther, until he finally found the perfect ladder on which to climb to success: Sue Ellen Chatworth, a plain and docile young woman who had spent her life trying to atone for having been born a female.

The elder Chatworths, including the much revered Daddy himself, had never paid attention to Sue Ellen. She was regarded as a bit of an error, a botched first try at producing a son. All their attention was focused on the point in the future when they would be blessed with their rightful heir.

After two heirless decades, during which time the daughter of the house attempted invisibility and was by and large raised by the servants, it finally dawned on the Chatworths that Sue Ellen and chewing gum were to be their only products.

Upon realizing this, Mrs. Chatworth quietly died of shame.

Given that Mr. Chatworth's entire existence was devoted to chewing gum, he was naturally made of more resilient material than his spouse had been. He came home from his wife's funeral and looked toward the horizons. As soon, he made it clear, as a decent period of mourning was over, he'd start afresh with a new brood mare.

But before he found a woman with the look of unborn sons in her, Ellsworth Hummer appeared and became the first human being to take Sue Ellen seriously. She was, understandably, dazzled. Her father took a dimmer view of the courtship.

He was not for a moment enchanted when Ellsworth appeared at his office door and formally asked for Sue Ellen's hand. "Blackguard!" he shouted. "Fortune hunter!"

Ellsworth merely grinned. "Now, now," he said. "You won't be losing a daughter. You'll be gaining a son at long last."

Mr. Chatworth was unused to either irony or defiance in even the most minute dosages. His veins expanded dangerously. His face became mauve, a color Ellsworth had never particularly cared for. Short of breath, he waved his fist at the young man on the other side of his desk. "You'll get *nothing!* I'll change my will!" he shouted. "If you and that daughter of mine, that—"

"Sue Ellen," Ellsworth prompted. "Sue Ellen's her name, Pop."

Mr. Chatworth was now the color of a fully mature egg-plant. "I'll see that you don't get what you want if it's the last thing I—"

"We were thinking of having the wedding in about two weeks," Ellsworth said mildly. "I'd like you to give your daughter away, of course."

"You'll marry over my dead body!" Mr. Chatworth shouted. And then he toppled, facedown, onto his desk and ceased this life thereby, as ever, proving himself correct and having the last word on the subject.

Grateful that the gods and high blood pressure had conspired to pave his way, Ellsworth sailed into marriage and a chewing gum empire. But a mere six months later, he recognized that his triumph was hollow. A sham. All he'd truly gotten was married. Very. And Sue Ellen thought that meant something, wanted to be close to him, seemed unable to comprehend that she was merely a means to an end, to the stock, to the money.

At each of the six monthly board meetings, Ellsworth wheedled, cajoled, charmed, argued and pontificated about the necessity of his being given some real control. During six months' worth of non-board meeting days, Ellsworth suggested, hinted, insinuated and said outright how much more of a man he'd feel if Sue Ellen would only treat him as an equal.

"Oh, honey," Sue Ellen would giggle from her pillow, "you're more than enough of a man for me already!"

Today's board meeting had been his last attempt. Now there was no remedy left except Sue Ellen's death.

But how?

Every eye in the impossibly tight-knit family would be on him. He needed a rock-solid alibi. No amateurish hacking or burying in the cellar would work. The cousins detested him

76

as actively as he disliked them. He had to remain above suspicion.

"Hi, Ellsworth," Sue Ellen said brightly, interrupting his dark and private thoughts. "You working in here or something?"

"What work would I be doing?" he said. "What real work do I have to do?"

"Still sulking? Oh, my, honey, you don't want to be so glum about everything. After all, we've got each other and our health."

He was not cheered by being reminded of those truisms. "You and your cousins take care of all your business?" he asked tartly.

She nodded.

"Anything special?"

She lit a cigarette. "Oh, the company picnic plans and . . . you know, this and that. Ellsworth, honey, you yourself said you weren't and never would be interested in the kind of stuff that concerns the board, and I respect that." She inhaled deeply.

"Those cigarettes will kill you," he muttered. But too slowly, he added to himself. Much too slowly.

"Aren't you the most considerate groom a girl could have?" she chirruped. "I know I have to stop, but maybe in a bit. Not right now. I'm a little too tense to think about it."

"Your family would make anybody tense," he said. "I hate them."

"Yes. I know that. But I like them." She had been leaning on the edge of his desk, but now she stood straight, then bent to stub out her cigarette in his otherwise unused ashtray. "I'm going to visit Cousin Tina this afternoon," she said. "She's been feeling poorly."

There was nothing newsworthy about either Tina's health

or the weekly visit. Sue Ellen saw her crotchety cousin every Saturday afternoon. "Goodbye, Sue Ellen," he said.

"See you," she answered with a wave.

Studying the effects of more brandy, Ellsworth listened as his wife's car pulled out, beginning its way over the mountain pass to her cousin's. And he smiled, because Sue Ellen had just helped him decide the method of her death. She would meet her end in a tragic crash going down that mountain. A little tinkering with the brakes and the car would be too far gone after plummeting over the side for anyone to bother investigating.

Ellsworth had one week left before he became a widower. For seven days, he was almost polite to his wife, providing her with fond final memories of him. He kissed her goodbye on the morning of the last day.

"Goodbye, Sue Ellen," he said, and he repeated the words to himself several times during the day as he lay dreaming of how he'd spend the Chatworth fortune. He smiled as he dozed, waiting for the police to arrive and announce the accident.

"Ellsworth!" The voice was agitated, feminine and definitely Sue Ellen's. He opened one eye and saw her. The dull, drab, infinitely boring, and incredibly rich Sue Ellen was intact.

"You'll never believe what happened to me!"

"Try me," he said slowly.

"I was going over the pass and suddenly I didn't have any brakes! I just screamed and panicked and knew that I was going to die!"

Ellsworth sat up. So far, it was exactly as he'd planned it. Except for this part, with her standing here, very much alive. "What did you do, Sue Ellen?" For once, he was honestly interested in what she had to say.

"Don't laugh, but I lost my head and screamed for my daddy. 'Daddy! Daddy! Help me!' like a real idiot, I guess, or something. But then, like magic, suddenly I could *hear* him, clear as day, a voice from beyond shouting and impatient with me the way he always was. It was mystical almost, Ellsworth, like he was right there with me screaming, 'Don't be such an all-around idiot, girl, and don't *bother* me! Get a grip and leave me out of this!' It almost makes you believe, doesn't it?" She looked bedazzled.

"Well, what good is it to be told to get a grip?" Ellsworth asked.

"What good? Well, I always did what my Daddy said. So I got a grip—on the steering wheel. I stopped waving my arms and being crazy, that's what. And to tell you the truth, I think that's what my . . . my heavenly *vision* meant, because what else could I have gripped? That message from my dear daddy saved me, because I hung on, racing around those curves until finally I was on flat ground again, and then I just ran the car into Cousin Tina's barn to stop it." She finally drew a breath.

Ellsworth tilted his head back and glowered upward. He felt strongly that supernatural intervention—even of the bad-tempered kind—violated all the rules.

Sue Ellen's bright smile flashed and then faded almost immediately. "I pretty much wrecked it, though," she said.

"The barn?"

"That, too. I meant the car. I think they're both totaled. I have Cousin Tina's car right now."

Ellsworth mentally deducted the cost of a car and Tina's new barn from the inheritance he'd receive as soon as he came up with a second, more reliable plan for her disposal.

He was appalled by how few really good ways there were to safely murder anyone. He studied mystery magazines and books about criminals and was depressed and discouraged by the fact that the murderer was too often apprehended. It seemed to him that the most successful homicides were those semi-random drive-by shootings that seemed to happen in great uninvestigated clusters, but they were so urban, and Ellsworth and Sue Ellen lived nestled in rural rolling hills, not a street corner within shooting distance. Gang warfare would be too much of a stretch in the sticks.

The problem was, once the crime grew more deliberate and focused, there were horrifyingly accurate ways of identifying the culprit, right down to matching his DNA from the merest bit of him. It was Ellsworth's opinion that forensic science had gone entirely too far.

However, accidents in the home seemed more likely to pass muster. People clucked their tongues and shook their heads and moved on without undue attention or speculation. So one Monday morning, before he left for another day of sitting and staring at his office walls, Ellsworth carefully greased the bottom of the shower with Sue Ellen's night cream. Then he dropped the jar and left. Sue Ellen was fond of starting her day a bit later than he began his. She was "not a morning person" in her own clichéd words, and she required a steamy hot shower to "get the old motor turning over." This time, he hoped to get more than the old motor and the clichés twirling. He was confident she'd slip and either be scalded to death, die of head injuries, or cover the drain in her fall and drown. That sort of thing happened all the time and didn't even make headlines.

This plan had some latitude, and he liked it.

He was downstairs, drinking coffee and reading the morning paper, when the old pipes of the house signaled that Sue Ellen's shower was going full blast.

"Yes!" he said, raising his buttered toast like a flag. "Yes!"

Soon he would call the police and explain how he'd found his wife's body in the shower, too late, alas, to save her.

And then he heard the scream. Yes, yes! He waited for the thud or the gurgle.

Instead, he heard a torrent of words.

Words were wrong. Words did not compute. Whole long strings of words were not what a slipping, sliding, fatally wounded woman would utter.

The words came closer, toward the top of the stairs. Two voices. Ellsworth tensed.

"I don't care if you're new!" Sue Ellen was behaving in a shrill and unladylike manner, to put it mildly. Her daddy would not have approved. "Somebody must have told you my routine. I *need* my morning shower!"

"But, miss, I wanted to make it nice. It was all greasy in there."

"That's ridiculous! It was cleaned yesterday afternoon. That's when it's always done. Well after I'm through."

"Messy. Greasy. But it's nice now."

And then the voices softened. Sue Ellen had a temper when crossed, but it was morning and she wasn't "up to speed" as she would undoubtedly say, so she made peace and retreated to her unslick, horribly safe shower.

Ellsworth refused to be discouraged. He decided to poison her instead, and he chose the family's Memorial Day gathering as the occasion. With forty relatives on his patio, there would be safety in numbers.

Cousin Lotta, according to Sue Ellen, was bringing her famous potato salad, just as she had every other year. Ellsworth had never tasted it, but he decided its recipe could nonetheless be slightly altered. He'd offer to help bring out the covered dishes. It wouldn't be difficult to make additions in the kitchen.

The plan was brilliant. Many Chatworths would be sickened, but Sue Ellen, her portion hand-delivered by him and specially spiced, would be sickened unto death. And if anyone came under suspicion, it would be Lotta.

He sang all through the morning of the party. In his pocket were small vials of dangerous this and lethal that to be sprinkled over the potatoes, and a special bonus vial for his best beloved.

"I'll bring out the food," he told his wife later in the day.

"Oh, thank you." She spoke listlessly and looked pastier than ever. Her makeup barely clung to her skin. Unwholesome, he thought. Definitely unappetizing. "I'm feeling a bit woozy. I'd be glad to just sit a while longer. Thank you."

It was amazing how easy it was to doctor the salad with no one noticing.

Except that Sue Ellen didn't want to eat. "I'm not really feeling very well," she murmured.

Ah, but unfortunately, left to her own devices, she eventually *would* feel better, he thought. Or was she suspicious? He felt a moment's panic, then relaxed. She was merely being her usual uncooperative, dim self. "It's hunger," he insisted. "You know how you get when you forget to eat for too long. You need something in your stomach. Sit right there—I'll prepare a plate for you."

"Oh, no, I don't think . . . I really do feel quite odd."

"You're overexcited by this wonderful party, these wonderful people," he said. "Relax and let me take care of you."

He watched happily as she ate Gert's ribs and Mildred's pickled beans and Lotta's quietly augmented potato salad. He had known that if pressed, Sue Ellen wouldn't dare hurt her cousins' feelings by refusing to eat their offerings. He could see the headlines in tomorrow's papers. "Tragedy Stalks Chatworth Barbecue: Chewing Gum Heiress Bites

Potato Salad and the Dust."

Maybe he'd give the reporters Sue Ellen's wedding portrait. She looked almost good in it. "Good-bye, Sue Ellen," he whispered.

Suddenly, she stood up, horror and pain distorting her features, and she ran, clutching her mouth, toward the woodsy spot behind the house. He followed until he heard the sounds of her being violently ill. And then, slump-shouldered, he walked back to the party.

"Stomach virus," the doctor said later. "Comes on all of a sudden, just like that. Going around. Let her rest a few days. She's plumb cleaned out inside."

"I told you I felt awful," Sue Ellen murmured from her bed.

A few of the cousins also felt poorly. Too poorly to drive home, in fact, and Ellsworth spent the night in his study, trying to lock out the noises of people being sick all over the house.

He could not believe that of all the world, he alone was a failure at murder. He went upstairs and stared at Sue Ellen. She managed a faint wave of greeting.

"I'm so ashamed," she said. "Getting sick in front of everybody like that. Ruining the party. I could just die!"

Fat chance, he thought as he watched her drift back to sleep.

Finally, Sue Ellen regained her strength and began to visit her cousins again. They had a new source of conversation besides each other and chewing gum these days. Now they could review the Day the Chatworths Got the Stomach Flu. They also had a new project. While in residence, several of the cousins had noticed that the house could use some modernization and loving care. Sue Ellen had also become aware of needed work while she was on the mend.

"Falling apart," she would now say.

"Not at all! It's a fortress! They built strong and sturdy places back then," Ellsworth insisted. The sort of remodeling she had in mind would cost a fortune—*his* fortune. Even talking about prospective expenses felt like being robbed, or having a favorite part of his body amputated.

Nonetheless, Ellsworth did not have any more of a vote in the future of his dwelling or his inheritance than he did in the chewing gum empire, which is to say he had none. The house was going to be thoroughly redone. Sue Ellen had developed a yen to "do it right" to use her unoriginal phrase. She wanted someday to be featured in *Architectural Digest*. The prospective tab was astronomical. Ellsworth suffered each planned purchase as a physical pain to his heart, and eventually he refused to listen.

"Let me tell you about what we're going to do up in the—" Sue Ellen would say.

"Not now. I don't understand house things, anyway. Besides, I'm busy," he'd answer.

And he was. He was constantly, frantically, obsessively busy with plans for shortening both the span of his wife's life and the duration of her spending spree. He had failed with the car, with the shower and with the poison. His mother always said that bad things came in threes. Perhaps that included bungled murder attempts.

People were dying all over the world. Was it asking too much for Sue Ellen to join them?

But their town had no subway for her to fall under. Their house had no large windows for her to crash through. Sue Ellen seldom drank or took even prescription drugs, and when she did, she was careful. A faked suicide was ridiculous, since she was so unrelentingly cheerful—aside from a bit of temper tantrum now and then, of course.

He thought he would go crazy formulating a new plan. He read accounts of perfect crimes, but couldn't find one that didn't hinge on intricate coincidences or isolation or strange habits of the deceased that had earned them a slew of enemies, all of whom could be suspects.

One evening over dessert, Sue Ellen and Cousin Tina chattered away as Ellsworth mulled over murder and watched the women with disgust.

Sue Ellen lit a cigarette.

"You ought to stop smoking," Tina said. "It'll kill you."

"But not for *years*." Ellsworth had not meant to say it out loud.

Cousin Tina's spoon stopped midway to her mouth and she looked intently at Ellsworth.

"Sweet Ellsy," Sue Ellen said, "trying to keep me from worrying about my dreadful habit. But Tina's right. I should stop."

Ellsworth watched his wife's plain little face disappear behind a smoke screen and he suddenly smiled.

The next day, Ellsworth carefully disconnected the positive battery contact in the upstairs smoke alarm. The change was nearly invisible. Nobody, not even a fire marshal, would notice—and if he did, it would be chalked up to mischance. Ellsworth lit a match, held it up to the alarm, and smiled as nothing whatsoever happened. And then he waited until the time was right.

The time was perfect three nights later, when Sue Ellen stood in the living room in her stocking feet, contemplating her brandy snifter. They had just come back from an early dinner with Cousin Peter and his wife. They dined out frequently these days as half the house, including the kitchen, was pulled apart and chaotic. Besides, it was the housekeeper's evening off, and neither Sue Ellen nor Ellsworth was much good at figuring out what to do in a servantless pinch.

"I'm exhausted," Sue Ellen said. "Between the office and the remodeling, I feel like I'm spinning. Can't wait till we get past these practical things and to the fun stuff, like new furniture and wallpaper and things. I just hate even talking about the plumbing and the wiring and the replastering and—"

"Then don't," Ellsworth said. "Why don't you toddle up to bed instead, and get yourself some well-deserved rest?"

"You mean you're just as bored as I am about all that retrofitting and rewiring stuff?" Sue Ellen asked with a yawn. "I thought men liked that kind of hardware store thing. Why just today—"

"Tell me tomorrow," he said. "You must be completely exhausted."

Thirty minutes later, he tiptoed upstairs. Sue Ellen lay, snoring softly, in the pink and repulsively ruffled chamber she insisted on calling the master bedroom, although it made the theoretical master ill. It was symbolic of the many ways in which he was ignored and undervalued. Sue Ellen's pet husband. He looked down at his sleeping wife and felt not a single pang at what he was about to do. Her brandy snifter sat, drained, on her bedside table, next to an ashtray with one stubbed-out cigarette.

Ellsworth took a fresh cigarette from her pack and lit it, then placed it carefully on the pillow next to her. Then he tiptoed out, leaving the door open, the better to let the currents of air flow up the staircase and fan the fire.

He stretched out on his study's sofa and waited. When the smoke reached all the way to him, he would rush to save his bride but, tragically, it would be too late.

Just as everybody had told her—even her own relatives—smoking would be the death of her.

Ellsworth grinned to himself. "Goodbye, Sue Ellen," he said, and closed his eyes.

The howl hurled down the stairwell, directly in to his skull. How had she awakened? Smoke wasn't supposed to do that to people—in fact, it was supposed to do just the opposite. The sounds from upstairs were loud and harsh and he closed his eyes again. In five minutes he'd go up far enough to burn his jacket. Then he'd call the fire department.

"Ellsworth! Ellsworth! Wake up!" The voice reached him from outside the study, but then, there she was. Without so much as a singed hair and in her nightgown.

The scream continued from upstairs.

"The house is on fire!" she said. "Upstairs. I already called the fire department." She helped him up. "You look so confused," she said. "You must have been sleeping very soundly." Then together they went and stood outside on the lawn.

"Sue Ellen," he said slowly, "somebody is still up there."

She shook her head. "There's only the two of us home tonight."

"But I heard screaming. In fact, I can still hear it."

"Screaming?" She looked puzzled for a moment, then she chuckled. "I tried to tell you! The contractor said our old alarm was unsafe. He made me light up directly under it and puff into it and he was right, Ellsworth. It didn't even make a peep. That's incredibly dangerous! So he put in these new electronic ones and now we have them all over the place." She looked back at the flaming roof. "Had," she said. "We had electronic ones."

They both sighed. But then Sue Ellen brightened. "We should look at the bright side, though. Maybe we lost some of the house and a lot of time and hard work, but we have our

87

lives. Isn't it lucky that the contractor was so sharp? And what a miracle—he put the new ones in today and they saved our lives tonight! It really makes you think, doesn't it?"

Ellsworth nodded dully. The thoughts it made him think were unbearable and endless, and only the whine of approaching fire engines finally distracted him.

"Oh, Ellsworth," Sue Ellen shrieked. "I'm a mess! The whole fire department will see me in my nightgown. I could just die!"

"Stop saying that!"

He began to smoke himself shortly thereafter, needing to do something beside pace the floor through the long nights. He searched wildly for a solution to his problem. He considered hazardous sports, but they made him nervous and Sue Ellen was, by her own admission, rather a klutz.

He pondered whether a fish bone could be wedged down somebody else's throat.

He considered disguising himself as a robber and shooting Sue Ellen dead as he entered the house. But he couldn't figure out how to arrange a good alibi for the time since the only people he knew in town were her doting relatives.

He wept a great deal, lost weight, and bit at his bottom lip until he had a series of small sores there.

Then one fine Sunday, sixty-four days after Ellsworth had first decided that Sue Ellen must go, Sue Ellen herself provided him with the answer. "Oh," she gasped with excitement as she peered out of his study's window. They had been sleeping in the small room, living in much too close surrounds while the upstairs was repaired. "Look," she said. "We have a perfect day for it."

"For what?" he asked, although he had long since lost all interest in his wife's babble.

"For the board meeting!"

"What does the weather have to do with anything?" He asked. "Besides, it's Sunday."

"You don't come to meetings anymore, honey, so you don't know. We decided to have this one on the river. Picnic lunch and all. Kind of combining business with pleasure."

"Well, then," he grumbled, "since I am finished with your kind of business, in that case, I'll see you tonight." The fact that it was time for yet another monthly meeting was incredibly depressing. *Tempus fugit* but Sue Ellen didn't. Two months gone and nothing had changed. Nothing whatsoever. He was still Ellsworth Hummer, possessor of nothing except a meaningless title, and the status quo might last forever.

"Nonsense!" Sue Ellen said. "We need you there. We missed you last time. Oh, I know you had your little snit, but you are still the company president. Don't ruin everything. Besides, it'll be fun." She pursed her mouth and burst into an ancient and boring song. " 'Cruising down the river . . . on a Sunday afternoon—' I can't remember any more of the words," she said.

Wait a second, he thought. Rivers were good things. People drowned in them. And with a little help, so would Sue Ellen, this very day. "Goodie," he said. "A company picnic. What a treat."

He whistled as he drove. The river, he knew, turned and curved romantically between banks laden with trees. If he could get a head start and place their canoe beyond a curve, away from the relatives, he could push Sue Ellen into the water and hold her there long enough to finally do the job. A few minutes were all that were required—probably even less. A person could only hold her breath for so long. Then he'd release her, flounder around, and call for help. Her whole family would witness his desperate attempts to save her.

After a hearty lunch, Peter asked whether they wanted to

hold the business meeting now or later.

"Later," Ellsworth said. "Always later and later."

"Ah," Peter said. "Are we then to take it you haven't had a change of heart toward chewing gum concerns or board matters? Is that how it still is?"

"I have the same heart I always had. Why change it?" Ellsworth said with a mean smile.

The seven board members headed for the river and climbed into canoes. Agatha said she'd rather paddle by herself, and the rest, including Ellsworth and Sue Ellen, divided up into pairs.

Ellsworth was younger and stronger than his fellow board members, so it was easy and fairly quick to get himself a wide lead and to station his canoe in the arc of a blind curve. He could hear the cousins laugh and call to one another just beyond the trees. This was good, because he'd be able to summon them quickly.

"Isn't this nice?" Sue Ellen said dreamily. "Wasn't this a great idea?"

He nodded and grinned.

"I'm so glad we had today together this way," she said. "For once you don't seem angry about the business or how we're running it."

"Well . . ." Ellsworth said, positioning himself. "Things change. People learn. Finally, I think I really understand what can be and what can't be and what must be. So goodbye, Sue Ellen."

Her Chatworth eyes opened wide. "Why, Ellsworth—" she began.

Quickly, he stood up in the canoe, but Sue Ellen instantly followed his lead, and her motions overturned the boat, throwing them both into the water.

The dive into the river was unplanned, but it didn't discourage Ellsworth. However, the hard clap on his head from Sue Ellen's oar definitely did.

As he sank, he heard her shouting. For help, he hoped. But then, he could hear nothing more as the pressure on his head grew heavier and heavier. Was little Sue Ellen really that strong, he wondered.

Then that and other concerns left him forever.

Sue Ellen shivered as she climbed into Cousin Aggie's canoe.

Cousins Peter and Jeremy smiled at her from their boats and then Jeremy finally released his oar from Ellsworth's submerged head. "Went well, don't you think?" Jeremy said as he righted the overturned canoe and, with help from Henry, pulled the inert form into it.

"Exactly as planned," Peter said. "Ellsworth was wrong, you know."

"Dead wrong," Aggie said with a chuckle. "He should have come to that last meeting, don't you think?"

"He should have given chewing gum another chance," Henry said.

"He blew it," Aggie said. Her voice took on a chillingly Ellsworth-like quality as she mimicked him. "I have the same heart I always had. Why change it?" She shook her head. "No turning back after that."

"We have a *good* board and we work well together. Look how smoothly this decision was implemented," Peter said. "Quite a pity he never learned to appreciate our strengths or how the system works."

"Your daddy was right, Sue Ellen," Oliver of Product Control said. "The family can handle everything itself, just like he always said."

"We'd best get back to report the unfortunate accident," Jeremy said.

"Yes," Sue Ellen agreed. "But first, I have to tell you one thing I surely can't tell the police. I'm positive that Ellsworth knew just what we were going to do and that he *approved*. He knew that he didn't fit in. He didn't belong. But in the end, he understood. The last few weeks, he's been so kind to me, so concerned, so *serene,* you know? Why it's almost like he knew the plan and accepted it. Especially today. Because just before I toppled us into the water, you know what he said, real sweetly? He said that he understood what must be—honest and truly, just like that, he said it. And then he said, 'Goodbye, Sue Ellen.' Makes you wonder, doesn't it?"

And with contented strokes, she and her cousins and uncles and aunt paddled back to shore. Once she looked over at her late husband, nestled in his canoe.

"Goodbye," Sue Ellen whispered.

THE SHRINE OF ELEANOR

Nothing was as irritating as not finding a good objection to any idea her husband had. "But . . ." Eleanor Morris spluttered. "But . . ." Still, for the first time ever, her cupboard of objections, complaints and oppositions was bare.

"It's a lifelong dream," Frederick Morris said. "You know that. Paradise on earth, they say. I want to see it."

"But . . ." Eleanor spluttered.

"It's our time, El," he said. "We've scrimped and saved and put off so many good things, luxuries . . ."

The boat. That's what he was talking about. The stupid sailboat he'd wanted for years. All those outdoor conventions he dragged her through, even the talk about building his own boat. Was it her fault she got seasick? A boat was impractical, not for the likes of them, and sailing, a waste of time that could be better spent taking care of chores and meeting responsibilities. Eventually, Frederick understood, or at least stopped talking about it. Until now.

Or, good Lord, was it about the stupid RV? See the U.S.A., all that nonsense. No way she was going to be imprisoned in a metal box with wheels on its outside and Frederick on its inside. Who needed it, anyway? No place like home, was her philosophy. She hated the funny way people talked in other parts of the country, hated the weird things they cooked, the stupid ways they built their houses. And why leave when you could see everything you needed on TV, anyway?

" . . . and no vacations while Mickeyboy was growing up or since."

"Nonsense—you always took your two weeks off, even though you could have gotten time and a half if you'd skipped them."

"But we stayed home. Painted the house or fixed the decking, which was important, of course, but all the same . . . now, the house is painted, the decks are fine, the boy's a grown man and I want to see Bali before I die. Let's do it."

"But . . ." She just plain didn't want to go to Bali. Didn't, for that matter, want to go anywhere with Frederick. Didn't want Frederick. "What about your cats?"

"Margaret told me she'd gladly take care of them while we're gone."

"She'll steal them, Frederick." Not that Eleanor would care. "She'll alienate their affections."

"Nonsense. She loves them. They'll be happy, and even if they run home here by mistake, she lives down the street, so she'll know where to get them. The Mickeys will love it."

"They'll be spoiled rotten by the time we get back."

"Cats are born spoiled. What's Margaret going to do that I don't already do? I've always had a soft spot for my Mickeys."

She grit her teeth. His Mickeys were pampered jerks, lording it around the house and eating only gourmet delicacies, costing them a fortune.

Everything about the Mickeys irritated her, starting with their names. Forty-two years ago, when she was a newlywed, a tiny mewling black and white stray that gave Eleanor the willies, but that Frederick found charming, the way he found every cat on God's earth charming, appeared at their door. He named it Mickey, because of its coloring. "Mickey

Cat, not Mouse, get it?" he'd said. "See the little white gloves?"

The Mickey joke was one of many early clues that her groom was not as much of a prize catch as she'd thought he might be.

And she didn't like cats. They shed. They got fleas. They ruined furniture. And they liked Frederick, not her.

He'd named every cat since then—and there had been numbers of them—Mickey. Mickey Two, Mickey Three and so forth. It didn't matter if they were black with white gloves. They were Mickeys. Currently, Mickey Eleven and Twelve lived with them, and Frederick still found the names amusing and the cats adorable, and she still found Frederick, his cats and their names, repugnant.

He even called their son Mickey even though his name was Stephen. At least, there was no need to number him. One pregnancy and childbirth was more than enough for Eleanor. Their one and only offspring was called, by his father, Mickeyboy.

Not that it mattered any longer what they'd called him. Stephen-Mickey, no longer anything like a boy, lived fourteen hundred miles away. Their relationship consisted of his having his dreadful wife send Christmas and anniversary gifts. Always in bad taste.

Oh, he visited when Frederick had the heart attack and surgery, she'd grant him that. And he even brought that witch of a wife and his ninny of an oldest daughter, but they left the second Frederick was on the mend.

She didn't care. Stephen had turned out to be too much like his father. Spineless, ambitionless, impractical.

And in absolute truth, she could understand his leave-taking when his father was disconnected from the machines. She, too, liked Frederick hooked up and inert. Not that she necessarily wished him ill—she wasn't really that type—but when the doctor said that her husband was in grave danger, that his heart attack had been serious, that all his gaskets and valves and pipes had to be repaired—she hadn't been exactly distraught. There'd been instead a giddy reaction the nurse called "nerves." Eleanor would have called it dizzy relief. Her marriage to a man with one stupid joke and jackets covered with cat hair had gone on long enough. It had seemed that nature agreed and was granting her a reprieve.

Except Nature reneged and Frederick recuperated. Became a fanatic about diet and exercise and keeping a benign outlook on life. "Healthier than ever," the doctor said.

Forty-two years tied to such a man was excessive. And the thought of traveling halfway around the world with him to a stupid island where the women barely covered their parts was unbearable.

"It's too far," she told her husband. "Bad for your heart. Too dangerous. The doctor would never allow it."

"But I already asked and he said it was fine. Just to take it easy, take it in steps, don't overtax myself. So I thought we could stop in Hawaii, and Hong Kong, and Singapore. And maybe stay a while in Java, too. Just saying the names of the places makes me need to sit down! Exotic ports, different cultures, a whole new world, Ellie."

"Ridiculous," she said. "At our age—"

"At our age we *have* to do things like this. We should have been doing them all along. But now—when else are we going to live out our fantasies, the things we've dreamed of all our lives?"

"I dreamed of staying put and finally getting some peace and quiet!"

"Bali is the very heart of peace and quiet," he answered.

"Not when it involves packing and getting on and off

planes and winding up in a heathen country with bare-breasted—"

"They cover themselves up nowadays," he said.

She thought he sounded sad about that.

"They aren't heathen. They have their own blend of Hinduism, Buddhism and animism. It's quite a lovely religion, too. It's a different world there—not just far away, but different. For starters, art isn't a separate thing—it's part of their religion, of their daily life. After working in the rice fields, they dance, they sing, they play music and make masks all as a part of their religion and their daily life."

Another jab at her, just because he had once had delusions about being a singer. He had a nice enough voice, she would admit that, but show business was no profession for a married man, particularly one with a child on the way, so he'd done the right thing and gotten the job at the plant. Was that her fault? Was she to blame that there wasn't time to work and sing, the way he said the Balinese did? That she needed his help in the evenings instead of having him gallivant off to perform in a bar or at a wedding?

"The Balinese live differently than we do," Frederick said in his mild voice. "Less competition, less stress. It would be good for me to be with them, to learn from them. Therapeutic. And good for you, too."

"Me? What are you insinuating? I don't need to travel halfway around the world to gape at happy-go-lucky natives who lounge around singing all day."

"They don't. They work the rice fields, work hard, but they—"

"You listen now, Frederick. I don't need to get away to escape stress. I wouldn't have any stress in my life if only you'd grow up and stop indulging in these ridiculous flights of imagination."

Frederick's chin looked solid and set. Forty-two years and she had never seen his face wear that expression before. "I am quite grown up," he said in his customary quiet voice, although it sounded steelier, more solid than she remembered. "And I want to see Bali before I am so thoroughly and completely grown up that I'm dead."

She tried out different avenues of protest. The trip was too expensive, she said, but he asked what they were supposed to do with their savings, anyway. To tell the truth, every time she watched the Home Shopping Network, she saw lots of fine ideas for those savings, but Frederick was becoming too selfish to understand.

She relented a bit and said she'd consider going if they were part of a tour. Travel seemed safer, easier and cheaper—and less confined to Frederick, although she didn't say that part—if they were in a group.

"No," he said. "I want to be on my own. On our own. All my life I've felt like somebody on a package tour. I've been one of the gang, the guy who goes along. But not this time. No leaders, no itinerary, no rules, no time limits."

He already lived with no time limits. Almost with no clocks. They'd tossed away the alarm clock after the surgery. The doctor had said that he was to wake up gently, with no shock to his heart. Worst thing you could do for the heart was to be jolted awake. Not that they had to be up at any particular time, but it wasn't right to live this way. Loll around, wake up whenever. Wasn't decent.

"I don't want to talk to people I don't like." He was still going on about why he wouldn't be part of a tour.

She faked pain in her ankles and feet, claimed arthritic damage that made walking painful if not impossible. The doctor—in front of Frederick—said that the equatorial heat of Bali would probably do her aches and pains a world of good.

She insisted that the diet in Indonesia would kill Frederick. After all, he was supposed to eat low-fat foods, wasn't he? Lord knows, his damnable cardiac cooking requirements took up half her days, and what did those heathen people knew about health?

"Did you ever once see a fat Balinese?" Frederick asked her.

She had never once seen a Balinese of any shape, so she kept her lips clamped together.

"Their mainstay is rice, which is fine, and vegetables, and tiny bits of meat. Tiny. And fruit. A perfect diet. Much better for me than ham and eggs or American take-out."

He was casting aspersions at her cooking. The doctor had made her change every single thing she knew and liked about food, just for Frederick's sake. Now, because of him, they weren't permitted to have any of her favorite foods. And no rest for the weary cook. No fast foods. Frederick required slow food. Her food, slowly made by hand. Frederick got to retire and lord it over her and her very kitchen, while she slaved on without a break. It just wasn't fair.

When they reached an impasse concerning the trip, Frederick resorted to guerilla warfare, telling everybody he met about his dream and the difficulties he was having attaining it, enlisting their support. This was extremely abnormal behavior on his part—he had never been one to complain or air their dirty laundry. She suggested that he was losing his mind, and insisted he see a therapist.

The psychologist said he was doing the right thing, letting out his feelings. That, in fact, bottling them up all along until now had helped give him the heart attack.

In the end, exhausted, she realized Frederick had boxed her in so that she had no choice. She had to give in. This was not a form of behavior she had much experience with. Her 'giving in' muscles were flabby with disuse, and ached constantly. It pained her to see Frederick tote home travel books. It gave her psychic muscle spasms to watch him outline itineraries, clip hints from travel columns and collect ideas from anyone he met who'd been in the general vicinity of Indonesia.

And although she'd hoped that time itself would take its toll, nature proved perverse. Instead of wearing himself out, Frederick seemed to gain strength and vitality with each day that brought them closer to the distant island world. "I feel young again," he'd tell people who inquired after his health. "I feel reborn. Invigorated. I have something to look forward to. The only bad part is leaving my Mickeys, but maybe they need a vacation, too, and I know they'll be well taken care of. I'm practically delirious about this." Eleanor thought that delirious people should be put in strait-jackets and carted off.

And then one day, when the lady who lived behind them once again asked Frederick about this wonderful trip of a lifetime he was planning, Eleanor began to think in a new direction, emphasis of that lifetime of his, and that trip of it.

Okay, she thought. Fine. If he was so eager to see Bali before he died, she'd grant him his wish. Both his wishes. He'd see Bali and die. Having had no other trips, and having no life beyond this one, this would definitely be *the* trip of his lifetime.

Frederick made all their arrangements and was pleased when he saw Eleanor dipping into the travel books stacked on the coffee table. She soon gave up, however. The books weren't sufficiently detailed for her purposes. She would have wait until she was there and she got the lay of the land before she could finalize ideas.

Eventually, they packed a suitcase apiece with lightweight clothing and took along a satchel full of Frederick's heart medications. They stopped mail and newspaper delivery, moved Mickeys Eleven and Twelve to Margaret's, locked the house, gave the neighbor who'd promised to water the philodendrum a key, and set off. Frederick was elated and couldn't stop talking about what was ahead. Eleanor was exhausted by the preparations, and by worry over the future of her philodendrum.

Hawaii was nice enough, although Eleanor wasn't one for sitting around and doing nothing on a beach. Hong Kong was neon lights, crowds and skyscrapers, and she'd seen those things before. Singapore was boring and scary, with fines for things like chewing gum on the street or not flushing a public toilet. Eleanor, who always flushed and never chewed, was nonetheless glad to get out of there.

They tried Java, particularly two enormous monuments, one Buddhist, one Hindu, built God knew when and still partly in rubble. Frederick could not get over the reassembled parts, the carvings, the massive size of the places, the years and years it had taken pre-technological people to build them, the story of the Buddha painstakingly carved in panels that spanned the huge monument.

Eleanor had nothing but contempt for the places. Their stone steps were so uneven and dangerous that her feet hurt nearly as much as she said they did, the figures in the carvings silly nonsense—a man with an elephant's head, of all things. What was the point?

They went to the famous Bird Market, where, as Eleanor made a point of saying loudly, almost everything but birds were being sold. Peculiar foods she wouldn't touch with a stick and hideous komodo dragons and panther kittens—over which Frederick, of course, went gaga. And as for the birds—most of them were *pigeons*. "For God's sake!" she shouted. "I had to travel around the world to see pigeons in cages?"

"Very expensive," the guide said, with reverence. He explained how they had contests, the pigeons wearing whistles in their tail feathers so that their swoops and arcs made lovely airborne sounds. A truly excellent racing pigeon could cost a year's salary.

"Back home, we call them rats with wings," Eleanor said.

So they left for Bali, a short flight away. "This better be good," Eleanor said. "I've had it with people who talk funny, and can't build a smooth staircase—"

"Those steps were twelve hundred years old," Frederick said. "People's feet wore those stones down."

"That isn't my problem," Eleanor said. "They should fix 'em!"

Bali would have no wretched stairs she had to climb, Frederick promised. And the cab ride to their hotel was pleasant enough, she admitted as they drove through green and flowering lanes. They passed a group of women in bright, tight sarongs. They wore towering tiers of fruit and flower offerings on their head.

"How beautiful," Frederick said with awe. "Just as it's been for thousands of years."

"You'd think by now they'd have heard of shopping carts and tote bags," Eleanor snapped.

And then they arrived at their hotel. Several times, she had to warn Frederick to calm down or he'd have another heart attack. He could barely contain himself. "I picked this hotel because it's authentic Balinese," he said. "Right on the rice fields."

She looked at rows of free-standing cottages with thatched roofs and bamboo rails and woven walls and was singularly unimpressed.

And when they got to their room, she became nearly incoherent. "Where is the *bedroom?*" she demanded.

"Here, madam," the small man in the sarong said with a bow.

"No, I mean—where is the *inside?*"

"Excuse me? This is your room, madam," he said with another bow. "Deluxe. The bathroom is behind that door."

"This is a *porch!* Frederick, tell him—this is a porch! Ask him where the *room* is!"

Frederick smiled. "This is a sleeping pavilion, Ellie dear," he said. "Surely you see the bed. Balinese homes are built this way. The high ceiling keeps it cooler and breezes can come through the open side. What use would windows be?"

It didn't matter what fancy names he gave it. She knew a porch when she saw one. He had condemned her to an extremely high-ceilinged hut with woven half-walls and no glass or screens or anything—except insects and animals who lived in the woven ceiling and grunted and chirped if she lit the bathroom light at night. And right outside the porch were the rice fields, a grid of squares in various stages of growth and cultivation, separated by raised grassy walkways. She could not believe that she'd come halfway around the world to camp out in an infested hut on a field.

Frederick was enchanted by everything, no matter how ridiculous. "Look there," Frederick said the next morning. He stood at what should have been a window, but was instead open space overlooking the rice fields. "The duck herder. I read about that, but it seemed too unbelievable. Never thought I'd see it for myself."

Outside, an ancient man made his way across the rice fields. He carried a pole with a bright banner attached. A flock of brown ducks followed him until he planted his flag in the middle of an empty-looking field. "They'll eat the last bits of loose grain that didn't get harvested," Frederick explained.

The old man walked away. The ducks stayed in the field,

near the flag. "They'll stay there all day, until he comes and leads them back," Frederick said. "Isn't that incredible? Isn't it charming? Exactly what I'd hoped for. I don't know if I've ever been happier. I want to stay here forever."

"It already feels like forever," Eleanor snarled. "If I'd wanted to visit a farm, I could have gone to Iowa." Her sleep had been torn to shreds by the bleats and snorts and barks and moos, crows and bellows of dogs, roosters, cows, birds, frogs and possibly the old man's ducks.

In the light of dawn, with yet another chorus of roosters deafening her, it had become painfully obvious that this unbearable trip—and Frederick—had to be terminated as quickly as possible.

The logistics of ending Frederick were tricky, however. For a moment, she was optimistic about the night noises. The squeaking, squealing barnyard outside had startled her awake a dozen times, in precisely the manner that supposedly would do Frederick in.

But the calls of the wild outside their porch did not jolt Frederick. The few times their sounds roused him, he seemed delighted, chuckling at the cackles and caws.

As the days rolled on, hot and boring and impossibly foreign, she searched for other options. Aside from the insanely reckless driving that took place on the main street—the only street as far as she could tell—Bali was entirely too mild for murder. The people seemed constitutionally incapable of it, with perhaps one serious act of violence a year for the entire country, and that included acts involving foreign visitors.

Eleanor hadn't seen a police person since she arrived. That was the good news. Surely, if they existed, she could outwit them. They'd be too unpracticed to be much as detectives.

But the people in general were too smiling, too gentle. Eleanor was going to have to be mighty careful if she wasn't going to upset them with sudden moves. She couldn't, for example, simply push Frederick in front of a car, which had been her first idea. The passersby would notice. Nobody rushed, nobody scowled, nobody pretended you were invisible the way they did back home. Plus, the drivers, recklessly insane though they might be, were also tricky and quick-witted and would probably swerve in time.

For one wild moment, she wanted to disguise Frederick as a dog, because they were the single exception to the rule of gentle kindness. Nobody swerved for them. Nobody deliberately hurt the dogs—nobody here seemed to deliberately hurt anything. But neither did drivers try to avoid the mangy wraiths who wandered into the streets. Dogs were considered dirty, earthbound creatures who scavenged the offerings left outside to appease the wrathful gods each day. It was up to dogs to react quickly and scram.

For a few blissful moments, she imagined stuffing Frederick into a St. Bernard suit and putting him on the road where he'd be squashed flat by a careening taxi. Of course, she realized with regret, even in a land of reckless drivers and some belief in magic, this would be a stretch.

The long, lean cats who roamed the island, leaping up onto thatched roofs and staring down at Eleanor were, to Frederick's delight, not reviled the way dogs were. Cats were less earthbound, less crass, more celestial and discriminating, and they were tolerated with affection. And much to Eleanor's disgust, Frederick befriended a gold and white slip of a cat who'd taken to sitting on their porch and keeping them company. He even invented a new and equally dismal joke for this one. It, at least, wasn't called Mickey. It was called "Balicat, you get it? Instead of alley?" Frederick's sense of humor had not improved over the years.

She grit her teeth and wondered if a person could break another person's neck by swinging a cat directly into the jugular. But she guessed that even if you could, it would be difficult pleading that it had been an accident or a completely innocent act. She was living on a porch with no walls. She couldn't do anything that would arouse suspicion, raise Frederick's voice, or be observed by somebody gleaning rice out in the fields.

And there were no natural hazards to speak of where they were. At least none that she heard about or saw. They weren't warned against snakes, vipers, wild animals, or black widow spiders. Frederick was rigid about not drinking unpurified water or eating food washed in it, so he didn't even get a stomach ache. It was not a land of guns the way home was, so even if she could find one, using it was out of the question, let alone getting somebody else to use it.

She eyed the machetes used to harvest the rice, but they were really too awkward to steal, and what would be her excuse for swinging one, anyway?

The days rolled on. They took excursions to black sand beaches, walked the rice fields, watched men painstakingly carve masks. Went to the dance. To many dance performances. Too many. Night after night they sat on uncomfortable chairs around an ancient palace and listened to peculiar music and watched people enact old stories. Frederick was entranced by the diminutive, stylized Balinese dancers.

Eleanor found them excruciating. "They call themselves dancers," she sneered, "and they never lift a foot. Where's the pirouettes, the leaps? What did we pay good money for?"

Of course, Frederick had his defense and explanation. He was always on their side. Again it had to do with earth and sky, and good being above, bad below. "The hands," he said.

"Watch them. And the eyes. It's a different aesthetic, that's all."

It was no use. She knew what it was really about. It was about ogling dark-haired, dark-eyed, honey-skinned girls. Eleanor knew she looked like a piece of suet in this heat, her blonde hair slicked to her pale forehead. The Balinese didn't even sweat. Watching these performances was about drooling over tiny foreign slips of girls and then not liking good solid American bodies. Thinking she wasn't graceful enough, either, because she couldn't make her hands bend backward.

She was well and truly sick of the dancers and of Frederick and of being compared—even silently—to ten year old unsweaty girls. Even the damned cat was slender and the color of light honey, like a constant reminder of how large and clumsy she was. She'd watch Frederick snuggle and drift off to sleep, the golden Balinese intruder in his arms and a smile on his face, and she'd feel stranded and betrayed and she'd hate him even more.

One month into their trip, Frederick made an announcement. "I have never been this happy," he said. "I understand why people have always considered this paradise. I want to stay here. Forever. And try as I can, I can't think of any reason to go back."

"The Mickeys," she said.

"Yes. I miss them. But I know they're happy with Margaret. She always adored them, and vice versa. I'm going to write and tell her to keep them and to put the house up for sale."

There was no time left to dither. He had to be gone, and soon, or life as she'd known it would be gone.

And then, one morning Frederick decided to visit an old master crafter of instruments, but Eleanor, who could not get used to the sound of the Gamelan music in the first place and didn't want to hear what an old man had to say about its creation, refused. "I'm too tired," she said. "All this gallivanting. I'm not one of your ten year old dancing girls, Frederick. I don't have endless resources of strength."

He looked as if he understood. "Then rest up, dearest. I'll see you later."

"You mean you'd still go?" she said. "Without me? You're going to abandon me here?"

Frederick laughed, as if she'd made a fine joke, and left. Never, ever, had he done anything like that.

She sat on the porch, out of the midday sun, her lips clamped together with resolve. Frederick's cat, Bali, lay dozing on their bed. Frederick's books about this country, its people, its customs, its history, lay in a stack on the table. One of Frederick's sarongs, to be worn when visiting holy sites, lay on a chair.

Frederick was everywhere, but it wasn't the Frederick she'd known for four decades. Her relatively agreeable husband had disappeared and been replaced by somebody who lived precisely the way he wanted to, with no regard for her. Somebody selfish and independent she could not abide.

She had to find a way. A safe way. The perfect crime. The perfect weapon.

And there it was. As it had been for a while now. Across a rice field, near a wall, a skinny brown cat mewed in her direction. Eleanor was sure it was the same pesky cat that had nearly tripped her the day before. She had no idea what it wanted of her, or why it had chosen her to torment. But there it definitely was. Eleanor allowed herself a smile.

Bali opened one eye, seemed to consider the mewing, then sighed and returned to her snooze.

Eleanor, on the other hand, put on her straw hat and her sandals and walked to the market, humming all the way. The open-air stalls normally revolted her. What these people needed was a Supermarket with freezers and aisles and tidy stacks of cans and boxes. What they had instead were cramped rows of tables holding peculiar grains and pods and unidentifiable meat with only flapping awnings as protection from contamination.

Fish would have been best, but these idiot people didn't eat much fish. They lived on an island, but avoided the sea, and when she commented on the pure idiocy of this, Frederick, who thought they were so wonderful, explained again the religious basis, about how high, as in mountain tops, was worshiped, and low, as in the sea, was avoided. Demons lived in the sea. Hence, little fishing.

Eleanor surely didn't care why. Smelly, oily fish bits would have been the most effective. But she would make do, anyway. She always did.

A wizened woman with black-stained betel-nut teeth nodded at her, and Eleanor swallowed hard and pointed at a duck back. The woman gestured at other, more succulent segments of duck, but Eleanor shook her head and pointed again at the back, and the woman wrapped it in paper and exchanged it for a bit of money.

On the way back to the porch, she saw the brown cat. It kept its distance, but eyed her as she was sure it had done for days. It looked tougher than its kin, belligerent in some way. One of its ears was jagged, as if it had been ripped and poorly healed, and she could clearly see the outline of its ribs.

She had never seen anyone call it, or invite it inside a compound where it could find kitchen scraps and a child to cuddle it. "Hey, Mickey," she whispered, and she lay the duck back by the side of the path where the cat stood.

After a few wary glances and tentative steps forward, the cat seized its bounty and busied itself with it. Eleanor heard its purr as she walked back to her hotel.

The next day, Frederick announced that he wanted to learn to make batik, and he'd signed up for a five-afternoon beginner's class. He didn't ask Eleanor if she wanted to come along. Of course, she didn't—why ruin her nails with inks and hot wax? But all the same, he should have asked.

Each afternoon, for five days, while Frederick was at the workshop, Eleanor went to the market and bought a morsel of duck meat. She knew that if this were any other place in the world, the woman at the market stall would eventually testify against her. But not here. First of all, no one would suspect what she had done. Second of all, this was not a land of questioning and finding witnesses. And third and most important of all, Eleanor wasn't going to do anything. Her weapon would do it for her.

After she left the market, she looked for the Mickey—he'd be number thirteen, she realized. How appropriate. Each afternoon, she found him alone, slightly hunched and defensive looking, but less and less wary.

Each day she let him follow her a few more paces, and then she'd place his daily duck part on the edge of the path. Further from the wall where she'd first seen him. Closer to her room. The last afternoon, she tiptoed down from the porch, carrying her bit of duck, and placed it directly under the woven wall of their sleeping pavilion.

Frederick's batik class ended. He proudly presented her with a black and blue square of cloth, drips and blobs marring whatever design he'd intended. "Sarongs by Frederick of Bali," he said with a smile.

That night, the moon was full, casting a clear white light into the room, onto their bed. She looked at her husband and the Balicat curled into his arm, and she sighed. A tremor of regret stirred her.

But all the same. If she weakened, let sentiment take over, she'd be stuck on this stupid hot island forever. Besides, it was Frederick's own fault.

If he'd found them a more normal American kind of room with walls and windows, she wouldn't be able to do this.

If he'd been more sensitive and not left her all alone all these days, then she probably couldn't have spent the time establishing a relationship with the Mickey.

If he hadn't changed so drastically, they wouldn't be here in the first place and Frederick could have lived out his allotted time in peace.

With those thoughts, she got out of bed quietly, although very little disturbed Frederick's sleep these days and she probably could have clumped and thumped her way across the room.

She stood by the half-wall and looked out into the bright moonlit scene. The symmetrical squares of the rice fields looked surreal, green-black shadows pooling dark along their edges.

And below her, staring up with yellow eyes, was the Mickey, a smart little cat who knew which side his bread was buttered on. Or would, if this heathen land had bread.

Eleanor waved the piece of meat like a magic wand. She watched the skinny cat's head swivel as it followed the figure eights she made above it.

She put the meat on the sill of the half-wall and waited. She watched as the cat climbed the woven bamboo wall, nails digging into the dried fronds. When he was onto the sill, purring with anticipation, rubbing against her hand, Eleanor quickly lifted the duck breast and tossed it halfway across the room, onto the center of the bed.

In a single dramatic leap, the Mickey arced halfway across the room after it, and onto the sheet.

Also, alas, onto the Balicat, who understandably resented the pain of the pounce, the interruption of her night's sleep and worst of all, the intrusion onto her private turf, and expressed that resentment by a horrific yowl and a leap that tried to eliminate the Mickey who, in turn, expressed keen resentment of her interference with his duck fest. The cats screamed and hissed and spit and swung at each other, rolling, flailing and making the worst noise Eleanor had ever heard—even in this country.

Frederick sat bolt upright, gasping as the cats leaped against him, screaming cat imprecations and insults at one another. "What? What?" Frederick said. "Who—what?"

Eleanor raced around, looking as if she were trying to do something, taking swipes at the cat. "I can't stop them!" she wailed, just in case Frederick survived this, and she needed to look as if she had cared. "Oh, God, you're not supposed to ever be shocked awake—this could kill you!"

She was accurate. Frederick gasped a few more times, grabbed his chest and died, even as the cats continued to fight bitterly around and on him.

Eleanor calmly watched her husband's final minutes. It wasn't her fault that their room had no telephone with which to call for help. It wasn't her fault that as far as she knew there were no nearby hospitals, no advanced emergency techniques for heart attacks, no ambulances. Frederick was the one who'd wanted to come to a country were things were completely different from home.

Frederick's expression softened into one of great peace. He had, after all, gotten what he wanted. The trip of his lifetime.

And she'd committed the perfect crime. Her hands were clean, if a bit greasy from the duck meat. Who could they blame, except the Mickey cat?

Eleanor lifted the duck meat off the sheet and tossed it over the window ledge.

The Mickey was too engrossed in his battle to notice that the prize for which he fought would be his if he'd only leave. Fur flew and the yowls continued. Eleanor lost whatever patience she'd had. "Enough!" she snarled, scooping up the brown cat.

He writhed, balefully looking at her with yellow eyes, his fangs showing, his claws still pursuing the Balicat, and as Eleanor released him at the window ledge, he swiped one last time, leaving a scratch on her arm from her elbow to her wrist.

"Ingrate!" she hissed into the night. "See if you get another ounce of food from me! You can starve from now on for all I care!"

She put on a cotton wrapper and a pair of bedroom slippers and made her way to the night manager. "My husband," she sobbed. "I think he's . . ."

The gentle Balinese treated the widow with compassion and care. The hotel manager said she could stay, rent free, until the arrangements for her husband's return to the States were completed. Briefly, she considered letting Frederick rest in this land he so loved. He had said that he would love to stay here through eternity. But it wouldn't have looked right. This Buddhist-Hindu-Animist country buried their dead and waited years until they could exhume them when they could finally afford an extravagant send off into the next life, a lavish Cremation ceremony. She didn't care what the Balinese would think if she buried Frederick here, although there didn't seem to be any proper place to do it, but she did worry about what people back home would say.

Unfortunately, there was a whole lot of Indonesian and U.S. red tape to cut through, and the cutting took an inordinate amount of time. And even more unfortunately, during that time the conditions that had made Eleanor's victory so easy still prevailed. There continued to be an absence of advanced medical facilities, and so when the cat scratch swelled and itched, Eleanor applied the ointments she'd brought from the states and never wondered whether a land so lush and exotic might also breed interestingly different organisms.

It turned out that it did. And the organisms were as ecstatic about Eleanor's arm and vital organs and as ravenous for them as the Mickey cat, their former host, had been for duck meat.

Microbes move much more quickly than bureaucrats. Slowly, the red tape was sliced. Quickly, the microbes multiplied. Eleanor felt poorly.

On the day that Frederick's body was finally released to be shipped back to the States, care of his son, Eleanor, her plane ticket in hand, gasped, put a hand to her chest, and breathed her last.

No one knew what to do with her remains, which were in dreadful shape, given the appetite of those internal microbes. So in a last act of gracious gentle kindness, the Balinese kept Eleanor with them in paradise, buried on a hillside, halfway between the demons of the sea and the gods of the mountains.

After a while, it was said that the American man whose remains had been flown away had mourned the loss of Bali and so had returned in his next life as a duo of cats, one a sleek gold and white and the other brown with a ripped ear. Together, the cats and eventually a small tribe of gold and brown kittens, all with white paws, made the long trek to visit the grave on the hill each full moon, rubbing against the headstone and in an odd final gesture, using the marker as their private, gigantic, emery board so vigorously that as time went by, the stone developed grooves that almost looked like writing, like 'Miki,' but of course, that didn't mean anything.

The grave of Eleanor, the Cat Lady made it into the guide books as a tourist attraction. "If we believe as animists that everything has a spirit, or soul," the tour guide said one moonlit night, "we might think those cats—and perhaps her dead husband—had a bit of a problem with Eleanor, and are reminding her remains throughout eternity—perhaps taunting them with this news?—of how well all of them are thriving."

The tourists smiled at each other and were glad they'd traveled around the world to visit this funny, quaint country. What a great place. Had to buy a postcard of the Eleanor the Cat Lady Shrine and remember this funny superstition. Wasn't Bali adorable?

WHERE'S THE HARM IN THAT?

My mother always said, "Girls who are too picky about who they marry eventually find the pickings gone."

Luckily for me, I never had time to be picky, or anything to pick over. My prince showed up right away, in high school. Prince Hal, I called him, and I wrote "The End"—and a happy ending it was—to my personal fairy tale.

But I remembered my mother's warnings when I met Amber for dinner. Amber and I went way back, but since I married nineteen years ago, we'd gone our separate ways. She was a big success—her own company—image consultants, whatever that was. She was the city mouse. I was the country mouse with kids and a part time job selling glue sticks and appliques at Krafty Korners.

Every so often, we tried to find common ground, but it was always on "her" side of the city boundaries. Amber wouldn't dream of venturing out to the boonies if she could help it. That was as close as we were able to get to compromise. I was always the one who had to travel the furthest, literally and figuratively.

But it was worth the trip, as a reminder to me, because for all her sophisticated and glamorous life, her elegance and accomplishments, her travel and adventures—Amber was unhappy. You can bet that her mother hadn't warned her about being too picky, the way mine had. So now, as we stood on

116

the far edge of our thirties, the great forever after on the horizon, Amber was in a state of wide-eyed panic.

"Don't you know anybody?" she asked. Amber wasn't the sort to whine, but there was an edge of desperation to her voice I'd never heard before.

But I had heard the question before. From Amber. And I had searched my soul and Rolodex and hadn't come up with a solitary male who was single, straight, available and functioning. Plus, Amber wanted him tall. And solvent.

On her behalf, I had monitored my friends' marriages, searching for signs of rot, ready to pounce if they fell apart. But their marriages, like mine, seemed to have reached equilibrium, or simply a state of resignation, and not a one collapsed. Well, two did—George and Harriet's, and Merle and Paul's—but they didn't count, because George left Harriet for Paul, which rendered both former husbands ineligible for the Amber-sweeps.

"Anybody?" she repeated. "Where *are* all the good men?"

I knew the answer to that, not that she was really asking. She never wanted to hear about my life. Acted like it was boring. Like nothing happened. But out there in the boonies, that's where the good ones were, the ones with staying power. With me. And what was left for Amber were the boys you never had wanted to date, only they were old now.

Amber had tried them all. Scherezade's Thousand and One Nights were no more than a long weekend compared to Amber's accumulated nights and nightmares.

"I don't want to go to bars, I can't afford a marriage broker, I won't attend one more of those dreadful singles' outings—they're all women, anyway—or sign up for another of those dating services. They are absolutely the worst. I could tell you stories . . ."

She had. Hal said I had no imagination, so maybe that's

why I loved being told stories, particularly Amber's grown-up versions of fairy-tales about ogres and monsters and horrid things that lived under bridges. They were fun because unlike Amber, I didn't have to date the trolls.

Amber poked at her seared tuna. She constantly sliced, rearranged and mashed food, which, as far as I could tell, never went into here. That's another bad thing about staying single. Makes you think you also have to stay a stick-figure adolescent with wee budding breasts, flat-stomach, pipestem appendages.

"You have no idea what it's like out there," she said. "You and your perfect marriage. You're so sheltered, so innocent!"

"Just because I'm married doesn't mean I've been living in a cave the last two decades," I snapped.

"Might as well, as far as men are concerned. Have you even ever *known* a man besides Hal?"

"What do you mean, 'known'?"

"Hah!" She plunged her fork into the tuna and mashed half of it down. "I thought so. Your high school love, your one and only! I can't believe it. Little Mrs. Faithful!"

"Is that suddenly a crime? Am I on trial?"

"Sorry." Her shoulders slumped inside her perfectly cut suit jacket. "I'm jealous."

As well she might be. But even so, she had no business deriding my happiness just because she was miserable. She'd been too good for everybody who wanted her, until just as my mother said, the pickings—and my patience—were both gone. "How about ads," I asked, deciding that this was my last suggestion and the last time I wanted to talk about Amber's social life, unless it changed a whole lot. "You know, where you specify what vintage, style and special accessories you want."

"I couldn't," she said. "It's . . . demeaning. Tacky. Needy.

Desperate. And dangerous. What if they turn out to be serial killers seeking victims?"

"Why should an ad-placer be more dangerous than guys you get fixed up with or meet at work? Take a chance now and then!"

"That's great advice, coming from you," she snapped. "Mrs. play-it-safe. When have you ever taken a chance on anything more serious than a raffle ticket?"

I spluttered and protested, but the truth was, I couldn't think of a single time.

All of a sudden, I wasn't hungry anymore.

"Besides," Amber said, "the people who write those ads must be weird, or why'd they need to place one?"

I pondered how to phrase the obvious answer. Amber stomped all over my feelings, but I tried to protect hers. Because I had the benefit of a stable home life and true love, I could be more considerate of her emotions. "Maybe they're good people, like you. And they don't want to go to bars or join Singles clubs, like you. And maybe their friends don't know any good single women." I thought maybe that last idea was pushing it too hard because the world was crawling with terrific women who'd been dumped, traded in, exchanged, or ignored. The thing was, they were all around my age, and therefore invisible to men blinded by the thought of a perfectly stuffed bikini.

"And you know what they mean by 'long term relationship'?" she asked. "Overnight on the first date. It's all a lie, a fake, a come-on. I'm too depressed to try."

"You're self-defeating."

Amber shook her head. Her hair was the color of burnt sugar, and her skin radiated a bright heat, as if she'd spent the day in the sun, which she never did. But I could see her light dimming. Amber's fuel was a special kind of hope, the expectation that she'd get whatever she wanted, and she was running low.

Frankly, I was tired of Amber's self-centered romantic woes. I had a life, too. And worries of my own. Two of the kids needed braces, my part-time job at Krafty Korner was shaky, as was the business itself. And Hal worked too hard, flying all over and exhausting himself to keep us afloat. But none of that ever came up at these dinners. All we talked about was how she hadn't found a husband yet.

"I simply couldn't go through the ads," she said, "picking and choosing like a beggar in a used-clothing bin."

"Amber, sometimes you make me so mad, I want to shake you. If you liked being single, that'd be okay." Unfathomable, but okay. "But you hate it. You tell me you want to meet somebody, and you say it's impossible. I may be an innocent housewife, but I know you have to do something—flag down Prince Charming before he gallops out of sight."

"You don't know what you're talking about. Those ads . . . the things some of them want! The arrangements they propose! People like you—married women seeking a man for an hour a week. Or a man and a woman. Or a man and a woman and chains and sticky tape or God knows what."

"Not people like *me*," I said. "If you don't want it, you don't buy it. What's so hard about that?" She stared at me, as if she couldn't understand that basic law of shopping.

I took a deep breath and admitted to myself that once again, if I wanted something done—like an end to Amber's tabletalk—I'd best do it myself. "All right then," I said. "I'll do your searching. I'll read the ads, pick out only those that meet your criteria, and toss away the rest. I am a smart shopper and you won't do better than me. Beyond that, I have absolutely no suggestions."

She agreed to my clipping service. I wasn't surprised.

Amber was always happy to benefit from somebody else's work. "Only please, please," she said, "don't tell a living soul what we're doing. I'd die of shame. Honestly."

We made our list of particulars, what she had to have and what was optional. This shopping list was going to provide a whole lot more fun than looking for the best buy on facial quality tissue. I could feel long dormant juices activate as I thought about what was ahead. A hunt. A quest. A mission. A purpose.

I was thrilled to become familiar with the new language. SWF and DWM and ND/NS for nondrinker or smoker, ISO for 'in search of' and LTR for 'long term relationship.' I felt initiated into a secret society, and looked forward to each day's new paper and prospects. I'd save the personals for last and carefully examine each listing.

It was true, what Amber had said of me with such disdain. Hal, my One True Love, had been my One And Only . . . anything. Not that I've wasted time regretting that, or being curious about what else there might be. All the same, it became increasingly obvious that there was a whole lot else out there.

I discovered that the weekly papers, the alternative presses had even more interesting ads, and I expanded my research.

Even Hal noticed a change in me, and he wasn't an overly-observant man, if you know what I mean. "You seem . . . happy," he said one morning.

I was shocked to hear him speak. "Not a morning person," he had long-ago declared himself, and that had been that. He didn't do more than grunt till midday. It used to make me sad, to tell the truth. I wasn't asking for tap-dances and songs, just a greeting aimed in my direction. And the shame of it was, during the hours that he was talkative and interesting, clients saw him at business dinners and meetings. I didn't.

But you adjust, get over things. That's reality. That's marriage.

I kept my promise to Amber. I scouted and circled and mailed off the winners and never let my family know what was going on. I honored her shopping list, too, as I roamed through "Men Seeking Women" and honed the candidates down to those seeking LTRs. Of course, they had to be STD-free.

I also winnowed out the ones with bad grammar, like the one who wrote, "I love intimacy, slender and aware." No parallel construction, no shot at Amber. I also tossed the one who said, much too vaguely, "I have movie-star looks." He didn't say which star or movie, and for all I knew, he was a double for the raptor in *Jurassic Park*. Another wanted "an unblenchable spirit." I had no idea what it meant to blench, but thought it might involve turning pale and burping, and that didn't sound like Amber. Nor did the slew of men touching their 'child within,' which sounded unhygienic to me. Adios as well to the "spiritually evolved" fellows when I realized that both Jesus and Gandhi would have failed to meet Amber's criteria being neither tall nor solvent. Plus, they wouldn't have advertised themselves as spiritually evolved.

And since Amber was an inside kind of woman who favored artificial light and climate control, out went the excessively athletic, the skydivers, marathon runners and wilderness trekkers.

Amber wound up with one or two. I spent time with them all, the ones who made the cut and the ones who didn't. I loved speculating, imagining, discarding. At first, I was embarrassed. I thought of myself as—face it—the personals pimp. A procurer. But then I admitted that Amber was only an excuse. This was *my* adventure. I was doing this for me. Suddenly, my low-key life didn't seem at all without event and the imagination I hadn't had, or so Hal said, was getting itself born, flexing its muscles, having an aerobic workout. Where's the harm in that?

I sated myself with the outdoorsy and the indoorsy, with men looking for someone wonderful. Someone a whole lot like me, if you must know.

". . . looking for female interested in nude sunbathing and hot-oil massages . . ." Just because I hadn't thought about that till now didn't mean I wasn't extremely interested.

". . . seeking adventurous lady to climb the High Sierras and scale even more heights under the stars." I could be adventurous. It had simply never been suggested before.

But precisely what heights was he talking about? What hadn't I found out about? And was it too late to do so?

I took a deep breath and caught myself. I was a happily married woman. I had one of the only good men in America. Ask Amber. I had to squelch these thoughts, these immoral, wrong-headed ideas. But I couldn't. I positively buzzed with them, and felt more alive than I ever remembered.

I decided to bring the thoughts home, where they belonged. I planned a fantasy evening with my One True Love.

"Hey," Hal said after I'd kissed him. He held me at arm's length to study me, "What's come over you?"

"The children are asleep," I said in a low voice, "and you've been gone for days. Welcome home, darling." I was wearing a new nightgown and perfume. "I've warmed oil, and I'd like to massage your—"

"Jesus," he said, "what is wrong with you? All week, I've dragged my ass from city to city, waiting to get home and rest, and you want fun and games? I'm not a young man anymore. Do you have to make me feel bad about it with crazy demands?"

At first, his words hit me like a mallet. I felt crushed inside and out, literally. But after I realized that I'd been thinking only about myself, and considered how Hal must have felt while I carried on, I tried to be more considerate. I knew how fragile a man's ego was.

From then on, I kept the ideas I got from my reading to myself. The personals were my hobby, I told myself. Harmless. A diversion. I would never jeopardize my life, never hurt Hal and my marriage and my family . . .

But, what if there were no consequences? After I warmed up by shopping for LTR's for Amber, my eyes wandered from "Men Seeking Women" to the "Alternate Lifestyles" column. No LTRs here. No Rs, except of the most primitive kind. Instead, a meaningless—thrilling—universe of short-term encounters and experiments.

Dangerous territory. Off-limits. But I couldn't stop.

"Secure male seeks underloved lady for thrilling daytime rendezvous. I'm safe and full of energy."

Tears pricked my eyelids, surprising me, because what did I have to cry about? Underloved? A man was devoting his life's strength to me and our kids!

Full of energy. Well, in that department, Hal wasn't a contender, but it wasn't his fault. We weren't getting any younger. So it was shabby of me, unworthy, to moon over ads advocating boundless energy in meaningless relationships.

"Seeking discreet lady for daytime rendezvous."

These ideas! These were lazy, delicious cover-up words, verbal slipcovers for bad things—adultery, illicit business, the making of videos, the shameless baring of everything with a stranger. These ads violated everything I stood for, everything upon which I'd based my life. And I could not stop reading them. They were my reason for waking up each morning.

"I have a great sense of humor, am financially secure and I know how to treat a lady."

I realized I was weeping. I did that a lot, lately.

And I was speculating. I did that even more.

". . . fun. Are you as sensual and uninhibited as I am?"

"How would I know?" I asked the question outloud, heard it bounce of my countertops, the coffee maker and the hood of the range, echo back over all the years of my marriage. "How would I know?"

"Great listener," another one said, and my vision blurred. It wasn't that Hal meant to ignore me. It was life. Time. You couldn't expect nonstop romance. But all the same, ". . . I would love to hear your private thoughts and fantasies, or you mine. And then . . ."

And I lusted for an orgy of words touching more than touch could, of exploring the innards of each other's selves. Something I'd never known.

Then Hal came home, exhausted, the lines on his face deeper than ever, and I was consumed with shame for my terrible thoughts, the infidelities of my mind.

I vowed to stop, but I was too far gone.

". . . zest for life a must!"

More tears. I had a routine. I had a life. But zest? The only thing close to it was this, the daily readings, and they alone got my blood going enough to survive. Was that anything like zest? Was that anything like a life?

And then Amber called one morning. "You were right," she said. "Let me be the first to admit it and to thank you."

It seemed I'd "introduced" her to a "perfect" man, a widower with grown children, affluent, unencumbered, tall and

handsome. He was funny, she said, needing to tell me everything. They'd been dating for a week, every night, and he was
fascinating—been everywhere, knew everything. Loved to
travel and wanted her along. She knew it was going to last.
"And in bed . . ." Thankfully, she left the rest of that sentence
to my imagination. My fevered, overheated, hyperactive
newly discovered imagination.

"Consider yourself retired. With honors."

The newspaper was in front of me, the section with the
ads put aside, like dessert, for last. Except, my job was
done.

My hands trembled. No reason now to open the paper? To
read the ads? To live them?

Then the real meaning of Amber's call became obvious.
The ads had worked their magic for her and now, now it was
my turn.

So with a sigh of pleasure, I skipped the LTRs altogether
and sank into the featherbed dreaminess of alternative lifestyles. And then I opted for complete honesty. I stopped pretending that I was satisfied skimming the surface of my ads,
imagining the men and pleasures. I wanted to—I was going
to—experience them. And I grew amazingly calm—an exciting, anticipatory sort of calm—as if I'd been waiting for
this admission all along.

I went shopping. For myself.

". . . what you want . . ."

". . . what you want . . ."

". . . what pleases you . . ."

". . . what you want . . ."

I rented a P.O. Box in a different zip code so that neither
Hal nor the children could find out. And I carefully chose an
ad. He was discreet, knew what women liked, had boundless

energy, a pied-a-terre and a few free hours in the late afternoon.

I told myself that nobody would ever know. That I'd be a better wife for getting this out of my system. A less restless wife. That I'd stop making excessive demands, humiliating Hal, damaging his masculine confidence.

The more I thought about it, the more it seemed a way to help my marriage, because with my new knowledge, with my brand new sense of self, of entitlement, of my hitherto unsuspected passionate capacities, I knew that what Hal and I had wasn't much more than two kids, a long history, and habits. So, really, where's the harm in that?

The man responded by return mail, on thick, impressive stationery. Told me the address, set a date and time which were perfect, because Hal would be out of town, in Kansas, and he said he'd have chilled wine, hot oils and infinite patience and energy waiting. Those were his precise words. I know, because I repeated them to myself like a mantra through the next three days. And each time, I liked how they sounded.

I decided to dress the part, too. Go all the way with my fantasy. For the first day of my secret life, I bought a great black sweep of a hat that I wore tilted at an angle, like the heroine of a thirties movie. I looked smashing. I felt better than I ever had.

His apartment was in the city, in an expensive residential neighborhood, an area of weathered brick, climbing ivy, mullioned windows and great discretion. All the setting lacked was background music.

I carried a bottle of chilled champagne, to show that this was my idea, too; that I, too, had style.

Then suddenly, I was nervous. I rode the elevator, heart beating so furiously I nearly turned back. But of course, I couldn't. I'd come too far for that.

By the time he answered the bell, my throat and mouth were so dry, I was unable to speak.

"Ah," he said with audible pleasure. "You're here."

I kept my head down, the hat my last screen and defense as he closed the door behind me. The enormity of what I was about to do of what I was risking had suddenly hit me.

"Come in, please," he said. "Make yourself comfortable. I can see you're nervous, but please, don't be."

His words were soothing, his voice comforting, sensual and soft.

And utterly, horrifyingly, familiar.

My head jerked up, my face no longer hidden by the discreet broad brim of my hat, and I looked directly into the face of my husband. *"You?"* I screamed.

"You!" he shouted. "What the hell are you—"

"This place—this is your place—you put ads in—you—"

"What kind of woman—I thought—I trusted—" He went on the attack, as if I alone stood in a moral pit. Then I couldn't hear his words, only a roaring in my ears. This was *Hal,* my husband, my lodestone, he who I was afraid to burden with myself, my too-eager demands. *Hal,* who was too tired, who barely heard me but placed ads as a great listener with great energy, *Hal,* who complained about every penny I spent but maintained an apartment for his daytime dalliances. *Hal,* who was supposedly in Kansas at this very minute!

With each thought and pulse, my arm lifted, gained leverage and position until it—I—swung back, then forward, into Hal's temple, with all the weight of the very good bottle of champagne.

He didn't make a sound. Just dropped. Bump, like that, a look of amazement on his face as he hit the carpeting. It was lush, expensive carpeting, so he barely made a sound.

And then he made no sound at all.

Dead. *Dead!* But I controlled the reflex urge to scream. Dead.

I bent over him, but could feel no breath. I touched his neck for a pulse, then realized I still had my kid gloves on. I took my compact out of my pocketbook and held the mirror in front of his mouth. No fog. No breath. Nothing.

So I left, taking my champagne with me. I left the door open, so somebody'd find him.

Late the next day, as I sat in my living room still wearing my Krafty Korner apron after a hard day's work, the police arrived. It had taken them a while to track down who Henry Plantagenet, the name on the apartment lease, really was. Prince Hal.

The police were apologetic and embarrassed. "A lot of crazies wandering around the city," they said. "Your husband just probably took some foolish chances and . . . we're real sorry for you."

"I thought he was in Kansas," I said. They were very sympathetic.

As soon as I'd seen the reality of who was behind the ad, it was over with the personals. I was sad to give them up, but the good news was the discovery of my talent. Hal had been wrong about a lot of things, but the one that turned out to be most important was his low opinion of my imagination. I now knew that I not only had one, but one that worked a whole lot better than reality did.

Think about it—I'd been married to a figment of my imagination, a totally imaginary husband, for nineteen years. I'd spun a story about happiness with a somebody named Hal, and created my own reality. A virtual marriage, I guess you could say. And I'd been great at it.

That's when I started writing fiction. So it's fair to say that in stopping Hal's career, I kicked mine into gear.

I had and have no guilt. Why should I? I killed a man who wasn't there, a man who was a good listener with boundless energy and splendid technique, a man who knew what women wanted and respected it.

A man who was no more than words on newsprint.

He never existed, and he continues not to.

Where's the harm in that?

LOVE IS A MANY-SPLINTERED THING

I'm glad you asked to interview me. I don't mind that it's for a high school paper—honestly. *Sic transit gloria,* some might say, but I like young people. And maybe my story'll teach you—in time—that when it comes to women, don't believe your eyes. Or ears. Or any of your parts.

Never trust a woman. No matter how much you've done for them, no matter for how long, given half a chance, they'll betray you, each and every one. It's not nice to say, maybe, and it's painful to learn, but if it happened to me, then it could happen to anyone.

You might think I'd be bitter, wouldn't want to talk about it. But I like remembering the good part, the sweet times. I mean once upon a time, when people thought about love and romance, they thought about us, the Double Mikes. My half of the Mikes is actually short for Michelangelo. My mother didn't want to add another Billy Bob to a town bursting with them. But her choice of alternative was rather extreme, and being Michelangelo Stubbs wasn't easy in that backwater. My better half was Michelle, nicknamed Mikey. So you see, we were kindred souls beginning with our nicknames, long before we became bigger than life, the stuff of legend. Our names—usually abbreviated as "the double Mikes" or some-times, "Mike Squared," was used as shorthand, the way people use Romeo and Juliet, for romance, for closeness, for

131

the essence of devotion. "They're a double-Mike," people would say, referring to a perfect twosome. There was even a song called "Double Miking All the Time." It went platinum.

But you probably know this. We weren't exactly low profile. Oprah interviewed us, *People* held a Double-Mike contest for the most romantic couple in the U.S.A. and we were the cover of *Entertainment Weekly*'s "Love in Bloom" issue.

People were always amazed to think that Michelle could have created what became the industry that we called Romance, Ink. She was reclusive, happiest when she faded into the woodwork. Her natural voice was close to a whisper.

But she was good with words and no matter how shy she was, or soft spoken or afraid of crowds and public appearances—the book she wrote spoke directly to the hearts of half the world. And quiet little Michelle was suddenly the person everybody wanted to hear. In person.

An old pop song asked who wrote the book of love—and the fact is, Michelle did, and it succeeded beyond Michelle's wildest dreams. Or more accurately, beyond mine, because the truth is, Michelle's fine points didn't include vision or dreams. Michelle's dreams were tiny, pale and timid. That's where I came in—I woke her up and guided her into the world.

The book was called *Bliss 101: A Beginner's Guide to Romantic Happiness*, and you know the rest. It climbed the bestseller lists and became a permanent fixture near the top. That generated requests for more books, plus TV appearances, seminars, courses, workshops, licensed products, audio and videotapes, etc., etc. In the process, I had no choice but to become involved. It wasn't as if I was seeking publicity, or horning in on her act. Somebody simply had to help Michelle deal with what was to her the overwhelming burden and ordeal of fame. And who better than I?

Furthermore, I was the other half of the perfect couple. Not to brag or anything, but without me, not only wouldn't there have been somebody to write about, there would have never been a book, let alone all the rest.

Look, there's no reason for false modesty. The book was my idea all along. I'm not saying I begrudge Michelle one second of her fame. After all, her name was on the cover (it was my suggestion that we put it out that way, as if it were all hers) and her words were inside it, (even though I went over every single one of them and even though a whole lot of the ideas were mine.) I'm not jealous of the way she got all the attention, but fair is fair. There are too many people who act as if I was some kind of Johnny-come-lately, as if I jumped on the Michelle bandwagon when I was the one who built the damned wagon in the first place! I sold the idea to her—and it was a hard, hard sell at that. I put the ideas together and I just about *invented* her as a Personality.

It's funny, you know? Here was this book about romance, you see, and its hero—me—was this ordinary Joe, a data processor for an insurance company. Not the stuff of Hollywood movies or romance novels. I had always intended to be famous some day, but I couldn't figure out for what, or how. So there I was, waiting for fame while I punched in stats about bathroom falls and liability for Acts of God. I told myself things would change, but I couldn't see how they would, or why. I mean maybe I'd be promoted to supervise guys like me—but I never heard of a famous data-processing supervisor. In fact, my first idea was for Michelle to give me a different background in the book, so it'd be more believable that we were so romantic.

I was ashamed of who I was, and now I'm ashamed of that attitude. In any case, she refused.

"I'm not going to let you bully me on this, too, Mike," she

said. "I'm going to let the whole damned world know what a boring, phony, nothing you are."

She was in one of her moods, so she phrased it poorly. What she was trying to say was that honesty was the best policy, and she was right.

But it makes everything that happened ironic, because my ordinariness is what Michelle's readers loved most. "Hope for the terminally unglamorous" one review called it.

See, it meant anybody could have what we had. It was kind of a Clark Kent-Superman thing, this not so good-looking guy you'd ignore or snub just like everybody else did, who comes home to a dingy cheap apartment and a wife who's no great shakes herself. But because he is secretly a Prince Charming of the Modern Kind, he turns her into a princess and their life is enchanted happily ever after. Like don't judge a book by its cover and appearances can be deceiving—all that stuff. And all the other not so great-looking computer nerds and dirty-fingernailed grease monkeys who couldn't figure out why they should get out of bed and face a replay of the day before—and all their women who were never going to be movie stars—in short, the whole world—got hope from us. You didn't have to be handsome or rich or a celebrity to be sexy, to have glamour and excitement in your personal life.

What Martha Stewart did for the art of entertaining others, we did for the art of entertaining each other, which is, you have to admit, more fun and doesn't involve spray painting acorns, either.

If you ask me, we performed a public service.

We'd been married for two years when I had the idea. Michelle always said she wanted to be a writer, and in fact had written reams of things—mostly unsold—but she would have never, ever had the idea of the book that made her famous. Michelle had won some contest in high school, or maybe it was college, a *literary* contest, and it warped her, set her off in the direction of artsy-fartsy stories. You could starve to death on what she didn't make from them. She had no sense whatsoever—magazines would pay her in copies and she'd weep with joy and clutch the pathetic journal to her bosom. But man does not live on literary journals alone, so Michelle had a day job, too, managing the cosmetics section of a pharmacy. It was beneath her talents and intellect, and paid next to nothing, and I repeatedly urged her to set her sights higher, but she wanted to "save strength for the writing," she always said.

The writing she saved her strength for was not only a waste of time and energy, but it got the only strength she had. There were no leftovers. As soon as she'd cleaned up from dinner, she'd hole up in the bedroom while I watched TV and had a beer or three and felt pretty damned lonely, like what was the point of it all? A wife should have been beside me, cheering along with me. Isn't that what marriage is all about? But no—she hated football, baseball, hockey, golf—everything I watched—and off she'd go to the bedroom, with the door slammed shut between us.

Her literary aspirations—or delusions—were destroying our marriage.

And then one night she actually left the bedroom to tell me about an idea. She'd written a short story about a miserable couple—the kind of depressing story nobody wants to read—and it had kept growing in her mind until the couple was involved in murder. "It's a *book*—a mystery!" She sounded almost as surprised by the idea as I was. "About soured relationships and bad sex and dead-ends. So stop complaining about my not being a couch potato beside you. This will take at least a year of nights and Sundays."

She was not thinking clearly. The way anybody with

common sense would have seen it, there was nothing in this for us except a major rejection for Michelle and more lonely nights for me. She couldn't sell her short stuff, so what was the point of building a tower of babble nobody would buy?

"Everybody and her sister has already written a mystery," I said. "Who do you think you are? Grow up."

"Mine will be different. These people aren't criminals, they're good people whose marriage makes them—" She stood up straight. "I want to do it. I *will* do it, whether or not you approve. I've never in my life been as excited about . . . about anything."

You see how bad things were between us. I was less exciting to her than an unwritten mystery. Her little hobby had become intolerable and her delusions of grandeur were going to wreck our marriage.

"I can't let you do that to yourself," I said. "You're a sensitive person, and this will set you up for another depression. I see how upset you are when a short story comes back, but now, you'll make yourself sick for a whole year of working and cooking and cleaning and then writing—it's too much, Michelle, you're not a strong enough woman. It'll hurt you too much when this is rejected, too."

What I really meant was it might derail her. Michelle wasn't the most stable person, either.

And of course, she missed the point and reacted like a fish-wife. "Maybe you could ease my pain by getting off your duff to help with the housework!" The soft voice had become an air-raid siren. I was revolted by the sight of veins sticking out on her neck. But she didn't stop. "The only domesticated act you do is pop beercan tabs! Do something for me for once! For us!"

This is what I mean by mood swings. Look how she'd gone from happily excited to furious in an eyeblink.

I spoke very, very calmly. Why don't you do what the experts say you should—write a book about what you know?"

"Maybe I will!" she screamed. "Maybe I'll murder you, then *really* write about what I know!"

Pathetic joke, that was, and mean-spirited, too, but I stayed calm. "I mean, why don't you write about marriage, since you're so much the expert on how we should live? Why don't you write about how to keep interest alive in a marriage? Wouldn't hurt you to think about somebody else for a change. Or write what you already know—how to turn off your husband by hiding from him every night and hunching over a computer!"

"Anybody trapped in a marriage with you would hide!" she screamed. "Guess who *inspired* that short story! Guess why I can't get those miserably unhappy people off my mind. Guess why I started thinking about murder!"

I brushed off her words. It was that time of month. She couldn't help herself. But the words I'd said wouldn't leave my mind. I'd stumbled on an idea, the way great inventors do, and from that first moment on, I knew that if we could pull it off, we'd be on the gravy train. I also knew that whatever hell we lived in wasn't unique. We were too ordinary to be unique. We'd expected romance, love, sensual delights, pleasure. Only nobody told us how the hell to get it.

There had to be other slobs in the dark ready to grab at anything shiny bright. So if we could become the messengers of hope . . .

When Michelle calmed down, I explained it to her.

"I *hate* the idea!" she said. "It's fake, deceitful. It's a scam. It's slop and lies. More pop psych drivel. I don't even read that stuff. And even if I did, where would I find the happy couple? We certainly aren't love's young dream. The whole point of writing is to find the truth, to find your own voice.

Doing something perverted like that would destroy me."

One of the secrets of marriage as I see it, is careful listening—hearing the message behind the message—the unspoken one, and what I heard was:

She wants this.

She wanted to be a *writer,* but she was afraid of success when it was offered on a silver platter. "There's big bucks in telling people how to get happy, and since it never works, and they always stay unhappy, there's *always* big bucks there."

Michelle misunderstood me completely, I think on purpose. Said I was insensitive, hypocritical, brutish—dreadful things, and she had a writer's large vocabulary with which to say them, too. Things got to the point where after a couple of ugly sessions, she packed and said she was leaving, that she had made it clear from the day we met that she wanted to write fiction, that it was the most important thing in her life, that I was manipulative, controlling—all that pop-psych babble she claims she doesn't favor. But that's Michelle in one of her erratic, over-emotional mood swings. She was like a child, wanting only to do whatever she wanted to do without regard to how it might impact anyone else. After two years of marriage, the fact that my wife had a bad temper and no common sense did not come as a surprise, so I didn't let myself be discouraged.

Of course she didn't leave. Where would she have gone? She couldn't live on the pharmacy salary.

Eventually, after I'd explained for maybe the thousandth time—and getting her attention wasn't easy, believe me—I had to disable her computer to make her really *listen*—she agreed. She would write the book as fast as possible and get back to her mystery, and that would be that, and I was to never again interfere with her creative life. Blather, blather.

Interfere, hah! Like I said—it was the best thing I ever did for her. Look at the bottom line. Look at that cover of *Entertainment Weekly*.

Look how everybody on God's earth considered Michelle a writer. Wasn't that what she wanted all along?

And here's the amazing part. You look old enough for the birds and the bees. The book's success turned us around as a couple, too, made our own marriage more successful. It would be rude to go into details, but let's just say that before the book, I wasn't all that interested in carnal acts—at least with my wife, if you catch my meaning. Michelle wasn't all that much to begin with, and then, having her like her word processor more than me wasn't exactly a plus.

But once that book was bought and printed, everything changed. First of all, they polished Michelle up. An image consultant came in to get her ready for the TV interviews. Needless to say, she hated it, said she was suffocating inside a plastered on stranger's face. She was always a negative type. But she did it because we all knew it was the right thing to do. So she looked better, dressed better, and had highlights in her new haircut. (She refused to go for the breast implants we could now afford and that I suggested several times. Pity.)

But the mysterious part is that I didn't even have to see Michelle to be turned on by her. The sight of the book—its slick covers, the raised gold letters, the solid block of pages, the big pyramid displays in stores—every copy, every ad, every press release was a love-potion. A glance at the book was like seeing a naked, silky and inviting—and *famous*—Michelle who had been fused with every celebrity babe and world-class body (including implants) ever there was. I couldn't wait to get home and make love to her. And I have to say that even at the best of times, it had never been like that before. Never. "Famous, famous!" I'd cry at the crucial moment. We wrote the book on how to get bliss—and damned if it didn't work.

At least for me. The same chain of events stunned and numbed Michelle. She was too stubborn to admit that a good thing was happening to her. Just the opposite—every step literally sickened her. She did the interviews and the talks and the seminars and the workshops, but afterwards, she wept and said that the energy it took to perform exhausted her. We had to allow time in the schedule for her to throw up before every single appearance. She hated public speaking and she was too immature to grasp the idea that grownups sometimes have to do things they're not crazy about.

I explained the real facts of life to her—showed her the bottom line, asked if she wanted to go back to working in the pharmacy, and she dragged herself up to the podium, faced the crowds and shared the secrets of bliss.

The joke was that Michelle, the angel of heavenly sex, was too tired for it. Always. And there I was, dying for her. Life is strange and cruel—and so are women.

And despite what I'd said, she still threatened to quit, to plug up the money flow and cut off her nose to spite both of our faces. She did nothing except appear and complain and hole up in her room and write whatever was next. It was up to me to make every single arrangement and drive her to each speaking engagement and to then stay with her so she didn't bolt. Finally, I had to resign from my job and make Michelle my lifework.

Now always up close to her, I could sense when her motor started to slow down and creak, and I knew about how she was sleeping all the time when she wasn't performing or writing—always writing—the workshop diaries (Journaling for Bliss) and gift books (A Blissful Thought A Day, et al). I was worried about the state of her health, her general decline, including her temper. She'd tell me to leave her alone, but of course, that was the last thing I would have done. Instead, I became "proactive," easing her burden by officially making us a couple's act. There was no way I could abandon her or make her shoulder the entire load. I was up there only to catch her if she fell—literally or figuratively, and to help her answer questions when she choked up or tired, which was often.

By now I was medicating her for depression, exhaustion and such. The doctor and I decided to slip it into her food because she was too bullheaded to admit she needed help. She said all she needed was a vacation from me but those irrational tantrums were symptomatic of her delicate emotional and physical state. In any case, my becoming more visible seemed natural and right. Vicious people accused me of horning in on her, smothering her, stealing her thunder, needing to get a life of my own. One viperous columnist called me a fungus destroying an otherwise healthy plant. And poor, sick Michelle said she agreed, that her life had become one long hell. Just to show how out of touch with reality she was, she said this while we were sitting in our suite at the Ritz. Did she prefer our former one-bedroom bathed by the fumes of the freeway? Was that less hellish than room service and gigantic marble bathrooms?

I alone knew how desperately Michelle needed me to keep her steady. She was fragile, increasingly disoriented, requiring constant assistance. The medications didn't seem to cure her, no matter how I upped the dosage, but we couldn't stop them—they were all that kept her able to maintain her arduous schedule. I found a new doctor who prescribed pep pills, and I added those to the mix. I would do anything to help my wife, to save her.

Publicly, we were a hit as a duo. Privately, we flopped.

Again, sad and ironic, because being in front of a crowd myself, being on TV, being interviewed—all that was as powerful if not more so of an aphrodisiac than the book itself had been. But on the homefront, Michelle became still more tense and lethargic, with energy only to perform and write. She met each deadline: *Romantic Exercises 101*, *The Bride's Romance 101*, *The Second Time Around Romance 101*, *The Golden Years' Romance 101*. Romance was everywhere, except at home, but isn't that always the way? The cobbler's children going barefoot, and all that.

I hope you see the bind Michelle put me in. There we were—all our dreams come true, rich beyond our wildest fantasies and *famous*. Is it my fault I'd become the symbol of the great-husband-lover? It was what Michelle preached—so if the multitudes wanted to practice what she preached—am I to blame? Is it my fault that our fans treated me like a combination of Elvis, the Beatles, and that male model with the long hair? Me! From ordinary Joe to Mr. Wonderful.

With a wife made of ice. An icy fury who accused me of ruining her life and trying to kill her. She had zero appreciation of the effort and attention I'd lavished upon her and her career and her success. Her. Her, her. It was always her.

And see, the whole program was geared to women, to how they could make homelife terrific. I had figured that angle out right from the start—that's why only Michelle's name was on the cover. If we'd aimed the book at couples, the way Michelle had wanted, we'd have bombed. Guys don't want to be told how to act, or told they should change. Guys wouldn't shell out a thousand dollars for a weekend seminar telling them what they didn't want to hear in the first place. But women will do damned near anything to get a little love, a little romance, into their life. Especially pay through the nose.

So there they were, millions of unhappy, unfulfilled women, looking up to one of their sisters who tells them she's got the greatest thing on earth going with me. And there I am, the only male on the horizon, drinking in the love potion of stardom—and nothing to do with the desire. The King of Romance with not a bit of it in his life. Is that fair? Is there a human alive who could have resisted? Supposing the one you wanted shunned you, but everyone else wanted nothing but you. For how long would you, could you, keep to your moral course?

It wasn't as if I got really involved. These were one or two night stands, nothing more. And if there were a lot of them, well, there were a lot of cities and a lot of those nights.

Eventually, I could no longer hide the fact that Michelle was not at all well.

Sales doubled. I was asked to do solo interviews. It spared Michelle's ever-weakening reserve of strength, so I was glad to oblige. Mostly, they were about male nurturers, guys like me.

I had Michelle write a book about it, *The Romantic Caretaker*. It did remarkably well and to my surprise, turned me into a kind of hero. The poster-boy of T.L.C., somebody called me. Needless to say, it didn't hurt me with the women, either. Given my romantic inclinations and my sick wife—it was more or less a public service the ladies performed.

Then, somehow, although I was nothing if not discreet—the last thing on earth I wanted to do was hurt my fragile flower—but somehow, Michelle found out. Found out a whole lot—names, places, specifics. Things even I'd forgotten.

I can't begin to describe how the possession of a few meaningless statistics and names transformed my beloved into a shrew. The names she called me! The words she knew! The energy she suddenly found! She stood on the terrace of our home in Malibu—her backdrop the Pacific Ocean, far below, and above her, the wheeling stars. Very romantic she was in layers of frothy Victorian nightwear. She looked like an angel with her hair wild and her face flushed—and she screamed. If we'd had near neighbors besides the fish at the bottom of the stone staircase, they'd have called the police. She was a harpy, a lunatic, turning reality inside out, looking at events backwards, fouling all of it into something ugly, something foreign. She accused me of forcing my adolescent dreams onto her, stifling her own hopes and artistic ambitions, of backing her into a corner and keeping her there, weighing her down with obligations she'd never wanted and couldn't stand, making her ill with what she actually called repeated *rapes*—her words for all those nights of love, those times I'd been so enraptured, so full of ardor!

Rapes! You see how sick she'd become? She said I capitalized on her illness after *creating* it and then abused her by "whoring around." She said she'd been *poisoned* with drugs and kept ill.

She obviously no longer comprehended reality. She even accused me of siphoning off profits and hiding them from her when the truth was, the intricacies of finance were beyond her, so I hadn't burdened her with the details of investments I'd made abroad, or how some of them hadn't exactly worked out. And what was the point of making her sign more papers? So I left her name off some of them to spare her.

I'd devoted my life to her needs, but all that was for naught, and she was vile. Michelle's betrayal was the worst I have heard of in the entire history of mankind, with the possible exception of Judas. I felt wounded, possibly mortally. All our dreams, the fame, the Double Mike fortune, I reminded her. We're a team. We're romance itself! "How can you destroy all that?" I asked.

"All *what?* I *quit* this lie, this sham!" she screamed. "It's my own fault. I sold my soul to the devil—*you*—to get you off my back, to leave me to my real writing. And then I let you force me to invent you in that book, the perfect man you never were even in your dreams. So maybe I deserved to be punished for deceiving the public, but for how long?"

"You're not making sense. You need to lie down, take a nap—"

"Get out, you no-talent parasite! You're nothing without me and it's high time the emperor went naked! Let's see how many ladies pursue you when you're a penniless, discredited, alcoholic, womanizing jailbird. You're going to pay for the drugs and the embezzling! I made you a household word and you'll stay one—but it'll mean something new. Goodbye Mr. Wonderful, hello slime. My new book is going to change everything you—"

I waved off her words. I didn't have to listen. The next book was about romance after children. Okay, we had to stretch the truth a little bit there because we didn't have kids, but then, we'd written one for senior citizens, too, and we were still young. Anyway, I didn't listen to the words still screeching out of her mouth. The next book was my idea, like everything else had been. She was just the self-important transcriber. But it was irrelevant now, anyway because she was going to trash everything I'd worked so hard to build. She'd said jail!

She looked like an avenging angel in that white embroidered nightgown and all around her I could foresee the disaster she was hellbent on creating.

For once, I couldn't summon my usual empathy, caring and concern. For once, I thought about myself. I knew there was no way to talk sense to her.

"You're *ruined,* Mike!" she screamed. "Might as well be dead as locked up in—"

A man can handle just so much stress before he cracks, gives under the strain, so I picked her up and carried her to the terrace edge with the cliffs and the surf far below and for a moment I held her there while she ranted, her words floating out over the ocean, to distant shores, to the whole wide world she was ready to snatch out of my hands—and I let her be snatched out of my hands instead. I tossed her down onto the stone steps and watched her tumble and bounce until I couldn't see or hear her any longer.

It was a tragedy, everybody agreed, her being so disoriented while I tried to get her off the pills she'd been sneaking behind my back—and falling that way. The terrace was glamorous but dangerous, with that open staircase. We put up a gate in her memory.

And that would have been the end of the story—the Romance 101 business had played itself out, anyway. What's that? No, I considered it, but there's a very small market for *Necrophiliac Romance 101,* so I decided to be perfectly happy resting on my Laurels—and my Juliannas and my Faiths and whoever else was there for me to rest on.

But in a last malicious act, Michelle ruined me from the grave. Not even death could limit her treachery. The book she'd been writing, the one she called "the new book" and babbled on about, knowing I'd assume she meant the one she was *supposed* to have been writing about postpartum romance—that "new" book was her mystery, the same damned mystery she'd been harping on from day one.

She could have—should have—told me, made that clear, but she didn't.

And she'd surely never told me that she'd named the villainous husband "No-talent Michelangelo," who uses his

146

wife's success as a ladder to his own, unfounded celebrity. Or that he drugs, manipulates, embezzles from and ultimately murders her. And is also a fool and a lousy lover.

Love Is a Many Splintered Thing, she called it. I don't think that's funny, or "wry" the way the critics said, but you know, I think they were just being kind to her because she was dead.

And Michelle absolutely didn't tell me that the damned manuscript had been sent to her agent—our agent—the day of the quarrel, her last day on earth.

Our agent didn't tell me anything, either. First, she worried over it, then hired her own set of detectives before saying a word to me. Even after they'd dug up whatever it was they wanted, she still didn't say a word to me, but she said lots of them to the police. And she turned over something else Michelle had sent her—a damned journal. Talk about not being open with your mate! I had no idea she was keeping detailed notes on every aspect of our life. Or that she'd also mailed in prescriptions, her detective's report, the names and addresses of some of the women I'd known. "For safekeeping," she'd said in a note. "Just in case anything happens to me."

I didn't have a chance. Because of a vindictive, mean-spirited wife.

You know what hurts the most? It isn't being in jail, or her betrayal, or the way I've been defamed. What rankles is that insult has been added to injury. Her book is Number 1 on the Best Seller List. For fiction. Meaning not-true, am I right? Not true, but her lies did me in.

And worse, worse, worse! She's famous again. A household word. Can't read the newspaper or watch TV without seeing mention or a photo of her. Or worst of all—full-color shots of the bookjacket with its slick soft pink paper and its silver and gold raised letters and her name in a large gold script and the full-color author photo of my Michelle . . . incredibly famous Michelle . . . I hear there are pyramids of those books in the store windows, and you know what that does to me . . .

Except she's dead, so it's like her one last taunt and rejection.

My point is—never give a woman an inch, son. You can't trust them. Take it from me, that's no fiction.

LET THIS BE A LESSON

The newspaper called it "The Cleaning Woman's Suicide," trivializing Claudia's death, making it laughable—but not to me. To me, it made it something to cry about.

Claudia, who'd hoped for a better life had leaped to death from the building she'd scrubbed, then robbed. Her suicide note was reproduced below her photo. In sharp-edged script she confessed to stealing electronic equipment, then wrote, "Prison would kill me, anyway."

There was something hideously wrong about her death and her note. Many things wrong.

Six months ago she'd entered an evening class I taught for adults who needed a second chance to earn diplomas and move on with their lives. "Don't expect much of me," she said. "My boyfriend Nathaniel says I'm too dumb to live."

Nathaniel was wrong. Claudia was exceptionally bright. But she was also illiterate, lacking even the basics of reading and writing. This was something she worked hard to hide her entire life, fooling teachers, employers and Nathaniel by pretending to be forgetful or foolish. Her childhood, I gradually learned, had been the stuff of nightmares. All her energy had gone into survival, and she'd had no strength left for learning.

But now, free of her parents and her past, she was desperate to finally become herself.

Unfortunately, her bully of a boyfriend wanted her to stay

"stupid," to keep her from "getting ideas" including—I hoped—the idea of leaving him. He made his points with his fists, although when I questioned them, Claudia insisted her bruises were from her own clumsiness.

Despite her past and present, she completed the first year's primer in one month, and skipped the next in the series altogether. She was a late in life prodigy.

Nathaniel's fury—with both of us—grew. He hated that she was absorbed in something that had nothing to do with him, even if he didn't know what it was. He ripped up Claudia's workbook and wrote me a warning on a piece of its flyleaf. "Watch out, or I'll teach *you* a lesson." His handwriting looked like a spike fence, each point emphasizing his rage, the force of the pen nearly ripping through the paper.

He won. Claudia quit, leaving me a note—something she couldn't have done a few weeks earlier. It said, simply: "It's too hard." I knew she didn't mean the course. I phoned, but Nathaniel answered and, hearing my voice, shouted, "Leave her alone or I'll teach both of you a lesson you'll never forget!"

The next time I heard about Claudia, it was through the newspaper's account of her death.

The TV news called Nathaniel her "grieving fiancée," but I knew him, and I'd known Claudia, and so I knew Nathaniel was the real thief and Claudia's murderer as well.

But what could I do about it?

Then Nathaniel looked directly at the TV camera and his eyes and sneer telegraphed me a message: "Taught you a lesson, didn't I?"

I realized he had. Actions speak more loudly than words, but he'd given me both. Nathaniel had taught me a lesson about himself and who he was.

I intended to return the favor.

★ ★ ★ ★ ★

Claudia's "suicide-note" was exhibit A. A blow-up high-lighted angular handwriting that perfectly matched Exhibit B, Nathaniel's warning note to me. "The budget I had for that night-school class didn't allow for new workbooks," I testified. "So I mended the one he ripped. Including the page he wrote on."

Exhibit C matched nothing else. "It's too hard," it said in careful block letters.

"Claudia *printed*," I said. "Nathaniel didn't know she was illiterate and didn't care enough about her to ask what she was learning, and he didn't care enough about books to look at the one he defaced. Otherwise, he'd have seen that Claudia's next assignment would have been her first lesson in script. She could not have written that suicide note."

A person should show respect for books and the written word. I taught Nathaniel that much of a lesson. If not, well, he has the rest of his life in prison to learn it.

AFTER HAPPILY EVER

Not that you're likely to believe anything I say, but the reality of it is that nobody should be the least bit surprised by what she did and how she did it. Assuming, of course, that you're willing to take off the blinkers, forget the brainwashing and comprehend that she did do it. All of it. That she has no heart. Never did.

The thing you probably don't want to know and surely don't want to believe is that despite everything you've heard about her from the cradle onward, she was and is a world-class bitch. Actually, she never lived in the world, so "world-class" is not completely accurate. She—and all the rest of us—live in what's called "Far, far away," or "Fairyland", al-though that is another misnomer because fairies are only one of our ethnic minorities and such gross labelling has resulted in a lot of bickering and factions. The gremlins, to name only one other group, have threatened to relocate en masse unless recognized.

The "once upon a time" place where we live and which we simply call, "Here," would more accurately be described as a parallel universe. Once upon a time is now. And then. And then some.

And forever. Ever after.

I say all this because I know earthlings like the sound of scientific precision. Like to believe you are in charge of the facts.

Yes, we know about you. Our telescopes and observatories are trained on you as a source of entertainment just the way your imaginations are tuned into us. We tell our children bedtime stories about your exploits as often as you do ours, and they are as charmed by your odd behavior as yours are by ours—although I think our behavior is much more *logical*. Try explaining the concept of "random violence" to a child who lives in "Here." You'd be laughed right out of the nursery.

I wonder if the stories we tell about you are the real truth (not that we are hung up on a single, knowable "truth" and science hasn't really caught on hereabouts.) I do know that the stories you tell about us—especially about my family—are fabrications. In any case, I doubt that you have the sort of PR people and spin doctors that we do, because if you did, your stories, like ours, would be more interesting, if you'll forgive my speaking bluntly. Where are your tales of globe-circling quests, transformations of gross matter into gold, boiling oceans, ice mountains, great and near-impossible heroic challenges and deeds, giants and trolls and curses and magical rescues and revelations? Where in fact is your magic?

Where in fact is your story of the dusty girl who cleaned the fireplaces becoming Queen of all the land?

Now that I think about it more, I'm sure the stories about you must be distortions and that's why they're so lacking in color, or at least have been since Atilla the Hun and a few of the Russian Czars. So perhaps I should be more forgiving of your tales, and I will—if you will also be tolerant as I try to clarify everything you always thought you knew about my family, so cruelly victimized by publicists and image consultants. And by their employer, my sister Eleanora.

Here's what you don't know about the part you think you already know.

There were three of us sisters—Eleanora, Lora (that's me) and my twin, Flora. You think you know all about Eleanora. She's a catchword in your world, the name for entire categories of wonderful, happy occurrences. Rags to riches. Sudden wealth. Eternal bliss. A Cinderella Holiday! A Cinderella Wedding! A Cinderella Victory!

How ironic. And how odd that none of you seem even a wee bit suspicious of her, given that she could never even get her story straight. Check it out—you have a slew of different versions, from Disney and his singing bibbity-mice to a truly Grimm version where the dead mother's spirit provides the fancy duds. And there are a zillion variations in between.

Aren't you people ever leery of a story that won't stay put? Don't you have liars over there?

The absolute truth is: Everything you heard about my family is a lie concocted by smarmy Eleanora and her tireless team. Their theory was that the worse we all looked, the better Eleanora looked. The sanitation squad is what I call her managers, although to give them their due, they're good. They've scrubbed her image and kept it squeaky clean throughout the centuries, and I'm the living proof.

At the same time, they've clouded my rep to the point where you're probably wondering yourself why you should believe a word spoken by the nasty and ugly sister.

And having said that, may I digress for a second? When and how and *why* did we become not only vile but *ugly* in your versions? Read what she told the Grimm boys. We're mean, but we're called "beautiful and fair of face." And then, suddenly, the story changes again and we're hideous. Isn't that overkill? Isn't that proof of her petty meanness? Does she become prettier if she makes her sisters uglier?

And we were sisters, too. It hurts, this step-business. We never thought of her as a hyphenate, a step-anything. She was not yet even toddling when my mother married her father, and she was immediately one of us, the baby of the family. In fact, that was the root of the problem. Mother was so afraid of the evil stepmother cliché, she bent over backwards and sideways and did acrobatics to make sure little Eleanora was never deprived of her heart's desire. Which is to say, the child was spoiled rotten, and we were all partially to blame for the misery created by the monster Eleanora became.

Eleanora. You hear that? Not once did I ever hear the name shortened, except when Dad lovingly called her "Ella sits-by-the-fire." I certainly never heard it reversed and perverted so that its bearer became a slave, a dusty scullery maid type creature that sat by—or was it in?—the cinders. Cinderella, indeed! Sure, she sat by the fire a lot. She was always whining about being chilly. Poor fragile wee thing, my mother would say. Baby couldn't wear long underwear like the rest of us, because it was too "rough" for her fair skin. Instead, she'd be wrapped in fine cashmere shawls and allowed to idle by the fire with a magazine and hot chocolate while the rest of us tidied and cooked and studied like normal women.

"What do you think you are," my sister once asked Eleanora, "a princess?" And Eleanora smiled smugly and said—even though she was so small and new to language she couldn't have—shouldn't have—been thinking of the class structure of the Kingdom, "I'm in training to be one." My parents laughed. For all I know, one of them taught her the line, but in any case, they were blind to how dead serious she was about it and they were blind to the accompanying outrageous excesses and because they found all of it humorous, they encouraged the delusions of grandeur the baby had from the moment she was potty trained.

It was an insult to suggest that she would have been required to do our scullery work. The actual scullery maid took care of it. All of us were pampered and privileged, only none so much as Eleanora. We were comfortable citizens of Fairyland with lots of household help. Dad was C.E.O. of a lumber business. That job of his was my only point of conflict with him. Dad spent lots of time deciding whether ancient forests could better serve as picnic benches and fences. The results were so awful that I sometimes think that what happened to all of us was retribution for the destruction.

But of course it was not. It was all her handiwork. Nonetheless, because of Dad, Fairyland was getting patchy. When young men were sent to find what lived in the center of the deep dark woods, they had to spend years searching for a big enough stand, and then to squabble over which one of them could claim it.

Unicorns, no longer able to hide or to wait for a virgin to spot them, are doing dray-work.

And dare I mention what became of the poor elves and gremlins and trolls and fairies? Deep, dark woods were all they knew, and once displaced, left homeless, you found them sitting on the sidewalks holding awkwardly printed pleas. A once proud people, begging. It's heartbreaking. The only time Dad ever raised his voice to us was after Flora and I picketed his logging firm.

Dad thought Eleanora still more wonderful because she didn't join us on the picket line. She said she was too fragile. Besides, she never joined anybody, anywhere. She was indolent and self-centered, and according to her, nobody was good enough for her. Besides, she would never question the source of the gold that maintained her lifestyle. And quite a style it was.

She invented a self that was so sensitive that only the softest fabrics, the sweetest scents, the most exotic ornaments were bearable for her fair skin and delicate sensibilities. Eleanora was an expensive piece of work, but everybody wanted to please her if only to avoid open warfare, for when Sis wasn't feeling properly and sufficiently attended to, the "frail" girl bellowed and trumpeted with rage. She wasn't above throwing (other people's) things or slapping and clawing, if she thought that would speed up getting what she wanted. A fishwife, a banshee, a shrew—whatever red-faced, howling, foul-mouthed image you favor. That was the baby of our family. Your heroine.

Of course, when we speak of her profound flaws and deformities, we're not talking externals. Those, her face and figure were outstanding, if predictable, even stereotypical. Hair like spun gold, sapphire eyes, a perfect mouth and nose, long lashes, skin like—you know the rest. Plus a tidy body. All of which items were chemically, surgically or cosmetically enhanced. Silicone up top, liposuction down below (we have all of it, too, you know. Costs a fortune. Only difference is it's administered without anesthesia in one second by a witch.) Eleanora was the first person in the entire Kingdom of Fairyland to have a personal trainer. Outside, she was sheer perfection. If you like that prefabricated type, of course.

It wasn't until she considered competing in the Miss Parallel Universe Contest (something she didn't get to do, thanks to the haste with which Prince Charming rushed into marriage) that she assembled the sanitation team. One of them must have clued her in to the idea that civility, even charm, could pay off, be worth the effort.

Although she never included her family in the exercise of same, I still watched with wonderment as she practiced image improvement with the determination she used to work on her waistline and hips with the trainer. I caught her practicing smiles and working with a coach to modulate her voice so that it "sparkled" and "pleased." And of course she succeeded.

She became a professional twinkler. She dazzled and pleased like mad—when she wanted to. Which was only when a person could be of use to her. When she didn't consider a person relevant to her long-term plans, she shut off the power, as if her personality was a great fountain in the sunlight that could be stopped with the flick of a switch, and as if she needed to conserve the water. Within a second, there was nothing left but surly Eleanora, screaming at a maid who hadn't picked up the clothing she'd just that second dropped.

None of which is to imply that I felt particularly sorry for Charming, when he mistook a professional cutie for a real human being. Frankly, the man's values were so warped he deserved whatever he got. Who uses a few dances as the basis of a betrothal? The invitations went out to every beautiful young girl in the Kingdom—and that in itself caused a lot of heartache to those who didn't make the cut. But "beautiful" and "young" were it. End of qualifications. What ever happened to brains or kindness or wisdom or talent?

Charming's father picked his mother, a former showgirl and great dancer, via the same good ol' have-a-ball method, and frankly, the Prince was a prime example of what happens when youth and beauty are the sole breeding requisites. Charming's bulb was dim. His drawbridge ended a few feet short of the moat, if you catch my drift. And I say this not out of sour grapes—Flora and I were invited, as you know. We were up to the royal standards of beauty. We qualified as Queenly material.

But what's to become of a Kingdom when all the Queen needs is looks, the ability to follow klutzy Charming (that's what we called him in grade school) without being tromped by his feet while you waltzed?

Or maybe it had nothing to do with dancing, just with feet. If you ask me, he didn't give a hoot about any of the above.

What interested him, what turned him on was feet. The man was a mentally deficient foot fetishist. A real catch, right? Don't believe me? Consider, please, the lengths he went to, the community resources he employed in search of the foot that fit that shoe.

Which brings us to the heart of the story. The shoe. Of course it wasn't a *glass* slipper! Please! Use your common sense. Even Fairylanders like a bit of logic. I ask you, could a girl dance with anyone if she couldn't bend her foot without shattering her shoe and lacerating herself? The same goes for the golden variation in other stories—you want a future princess to stomp around like one of your stiff-footed robots in shoes that don't give? To suggest, as some do, that the word mistranslated as glass really meant fur is to suggest that we are all idiots here. Fur shoes are for snow. They make the wearer look like a hairy forest creature—the last image Miss Fragility dreamed of projecting! And did you ever think of how hot such slippers would be, how sweaty-footed a woman would be at a ball held in mid-autumn when the nights were soft enough to hold an enormous party outside? Do you think the prince would have cherished such a soggy shoe? Would have searched for its wearer?

Those slippers were silver threads encrusted with *diamonds*. You should have heard the carrying on after Eleanora became convinced she needed them! It all had to do with the PR guy's thing about the need to sparkle but it also had to do with research. Eleanora knew a thing or two about Charming's quirks and that made drop-dead shoes a necessity. How else would she—literally—stand out in a mass of beautiful women? The part of her sales pitch that convinced Dad was that diamonds were recyclable, and that they'd be worn over and over by all of us and earn their purchase.

Do you wonder, then, that we were distraught when she

left half our investment and her fashion statement behind her at a party? We're talking considerable cash outlay here to coat her tootsies because her feet weren't nearly as tiny as the spin docs made them out to be. We're talking *lots* of diamonds.

Flora and my shoes were linen, dyed to match our gowns. Not that we complained. Eleanora was the designated glitteree. Dad, whose resources were being drained by his younger daughter, tried to believe in the importance of the shoes. After all, if his daughter married into the royal family, it would be good for business, Eleanora said. He was heavily in debt because of the diamond crusted slippers, so he figured that maybe they could also help him out of it.

And then, after all that, Eleanora *forgets* she's wearing a goodly portion of the family capital on her feet. Are we pretending a woman running on one high heel and one foot isn't aware of the missing shoe? Of course she knew she'd left it. And what dire event do you think would have happened if she'd turned around long enough to put the shoe back on? Nothing, that's what. But leaving it behind and rushing off into the night was dramatic, eye-catching, headline-grabbing and enough to drive a fellow with a thing for feet mad with desire. All part of her plan.

Midnight was *Dad's* curfew, you see, not some imaginary Godmother's. It was everybody's curfew in the kingdom, an understood thing, the time decent girls went home. Only some of us didn't make a grand fuss about it, and prepared to leave well ahead of time. Some of us weren't so single-mindedly intent on snagging the stupid Charming as to waltz on beyond the last song until the Great Clock chimed. And even so, we all knew that Dad would do no more than express sorrow and disappointment if we arrived home past his deadline.

So the deliberately dropped and ignored slipper was like a

smack in the face to the rest of us. And I think she meant it to be just that.

But by the time the story of the shoe and the royal search hit the news next morning, the footwear had undergone heavy-duty revisions. To our amazement, the slipper was described as glass. Diamond footwear was too *elitist*, the spin docs had decided. The people wouldn't like it. The people liked humility, liked luck to be a surprise to its recipients. It wasn't attractive to have planned and schemed and been given everything in order to get what you wanted. The people had to like her or they wouldn't be contented to remain impoverished villagers vicariously enjoying the glories of her ascendancy.

So glass it became.

And worse. A lumber executive was neither royalty nor the deserving hardworking poor. Not sexy, the PR lady said. So out with that. Since Dad couldn't suddenly acquire a title and be promoted, he was demoted to the more acceptable hardworking poor. A woodchopper. And a woodchopper couldn't buy his daughter gowns of gold and slippers of diamonds—or even glass. Hence, the invention of The Fairy Godmother as magical provider. Dad, who was still paying for the diamonds in monthly installments plus plenty of interest, found this insulting. He even tried to have his balance transferred to the Fairy Godmother, but the credit company couldn't find her address.

Our house was a problem. They couldn't shrink it down to the cottage they'd have preferred, so they did the next best thing and turned Eleanora into the abused, misused and pitiable resident of the otherwise comfy household.

"Ella-by-the-fire," Dad used to gently chide her when she indolently lolled by it, preening and lording it over us. He made the mistake of mentioning the phrase to a reporter, and damned if Eleanora, who was also there, along with her spin docs, didn't immediately twist the meaning of what he'd said. "Ella-by-the-*cinders*," she corrected the news copy to say. "Cinder Ella." And she gave the reporters a wan, sad but forgiving smile I'd seen her practice in front of the hall mirror.

The populace adored her. If Cinderella could literally rise from the ashes like a phoenix and become a Princess, then they could, too. They accepted every one of her lies, including the business about the pumpkin turning into a chariot! Tell a big enough lie and tell it often, and it'll be believed. It's true in every galaxy. I mean this one defied all common and uncommon sense—mice into horses? Lizards as footmen? Give me a break! But the headlines said it was so, the TV shows insisted it was true—and ultimately, it was. Sis even pointed at a half-rotted pumpkin she insisted was the actual one used that enchanted night. Then she had it cast in gold. Official "Cinderella's Pumpkin" charms became a fad, and she got a percentage of each sale.

We knew it was a pack of lies, but we were too trusting, too slow on the uptake. It took us much too long to catch on to the meaning of her maneuvers, to comprehend what her masterplan meant to us.

Very soon—the engagement was announced as soon as the shoe fit, and they married a few weeks later—little Eleanora was no longer a Princess in training, but the real thing. She took her diamond slippers with her, insisting they were now an "historic artifact." I have no idea what that could mean. It's a foreign term. We don't have history. It's pretty much always now here, except for the "once upon a time," which means anytime not exactly now, which is what all time becomes by the time you mention it. What I did understand was that she took the diamonds, all that we had left.

We lived quietly, almost as humbly as our sister's PR men

would have had people believe, although not by choice. Things kept going downhill for Dad, and Eleanora's ascendancy to the throne did not increase his business. The Princess said it "wouldn't look good" (to whom? This is an absolute monarchy) if Charming pushed business in Dad's direction.

And it was worse than that, because as Cinderella gave more and more interviews, her horrible lies about her past ruined whatever was left of our reputations. Dad's ethics were called into question and his business fell off even more. Mother noticed an absence of callers and invitations and Flora's and my social life dwindled to nothingness. Men we'd been seeing backed off and disappeared. People were afraid to associate with us, to be tarred by the same brush. Our house became a target for vandals. Paint was tossed onto it, and windows broken by rocks. And nobody cared.

We weren't even invited to the christenings when each of the two royal sons were born. I actually thought of hiring a woman who lived deep in one of the only surviving woods. She was known for the excellence and efficiency of her curses. But she was terribly expensive and we had no money. Besides, I didn't want to sink to that level.

Our situation became intolerable. We thought of leaving, crossing the Sea of No End and braving dragons and whirlwinds and the edge of everything simply to get away. But I hated giving up without trying a different route first, a last ditch attempt to regain the dignity and reputation that was rightfully ours.

I took the first steps in suing the Princess formerly known as Eleanora for libel and slander.

Now I must say that as time had gone on, although the people of Charming's Kingdom adored their fair Queen, Charming himself seemed less entranced with every passing day. I'm not sure what precisely provoked it—the new crop of young and beautiful girls, Ella's ever-more-expensive ward-robe, including her fondness now for gem-studded slippers, her mean-spiritedness, which rumor had slipping out more every day, or perhaps it was that talk of her dalliances with a wandering minstrel in a vacant spinning room.

Or maybe Charming had found a fabulous new foot. In any case, the rumbles and creaks of a marriage with dry rot were increasingly heard.

Eleanora was sufficiently distressed to pay her parents her first visit in years. She didn't precisely ask for advice or help, but she did say, with a great show of sniffles that she and Charming were having difficulties, that she feared he had strayed and that she didn't know what to do about it all, how to be a happy girl again. "Of course," she said, "I should be glad I'm safe economically. Royal families stay together. The mother of the future King is not to be tossed aside."

Well, we hadn't had a whole lot to do, impoverished and friendless as we were, so we'd been watching your planet's "soap stories," I think you call them, or is the term "the news?"—a whole lot more than was healthy. But they'd taught us a great deal, so that I was able to explain that in-deed, Princesses, even those who were the mother of future Kings, did get put aside and did lose their royal status. In fact, it seemed almost as much of a fad on earth as the pumpkin necklaces were in our neck of the universe.

"Oh, that's on *earth*," HRH Cinderella said. "Who cares what those dullards do?"

I thought she should care. "You're right," I said. "We don't divorce Here. Our ways of removing someone weari-some are more creative. The undesired—that'd be you, Sis," I went on, "could be turned to stone, or have toads come out of your mouth when you spoke, or turned into a warty crone or a flounder. Or sent to wander as a beggar for a thousand years. Or—well, why go on? We are an imaginative people, so there's an infinite list of possibilities, all much more fun than earth's dry way of dividing up assets and making settlements and such."

I must confess, I did get a nasty pleasure out of seeing Eleanora face a future as bleak and destroyed as the one she'd crafted for us.

For reasons of her own, Flora found that moment of silence an apt time to inform our younger sister of the lawsuit I had initiated against her. Flora spoke calmly, but made it clear that all the soon-to-be former Princess' dirty secrets and dreadful lies were about to be exposed. Maybe even photos of her pre-surgery self. Maybe enough ammunition to make the Prince put her under the worst spell ever devised. Flora commented further on how interesting it would be when we ultimately were all equals once again.

When Eleanora left, she was pale with shock. For once, Cinderella had listened to what we said. Perhaps, she'd even cared.

Now that was the part of the story you thought you knew, but didn't. This is the part of the story you've never heard. But it's all true. It's what happened *after* happily ever.

I should have realized that Eleanora's cunning and my naivete would make me a loser in any encounter, but I didn't think twice when shortly after the day at our house, she sent a messenger requesting that I come to the palace so that we could "talk our problems through." She said she had a solution to all our woes.

Filled with images of familial peace at last, daring even to daydream about a contrite Princess admitting to the world that she had fabricated an oppressed past, a Princess newly dedicated to protecting her family and introducing her kind and generous and upright family—to her subjects, I set out for the Palace in the family carriage (the one she claimed had sprung from a pumpkin shell.) I was admittedly eager to see the royal dwelling, the parts of the castle which tours didn't include, and to meet my nephews. I made my heart happy and expectant, made my eyes look toward the future rather than give in to the bitter undertaste that wondered why it had taken years to gain entry to my own sister's world.

After a tour of the sumptuous living quarters and a brief visit with the two young princes who seemed, not too surprisingly, vacant-eyed and appearing to be having grave difficulties with their schoolwork, Eleanora showed me to a special pavilion where she enjoyed spending time. It was up high, atop a turret, peaceful and private as befits royalty, with only the distant sound of waterfalls and the nearby songs of birds, with blue and white striped awnings providing shade, and great tubs of flowers that must have been tended by a wizard for I had never seen rainbow hued blossoms such as these.

A young girl brought us cakes and sweet chilled drinks then seated herself by the pavilion ledge to wait for further orders. I sat in airy comfort, and when Eleanora spoke, her voice sounded distant and disembodied, another melody for this magical spot.

"I am troubled, as you might understand," she said in a voice so sweet, I would have taken it to be from a stranger, were the servant girl not now asleep and Eleanora not the only other person present. "I fear the lawsuit almost as much as I fear being banished, stripped of my possessions and my sons and sent to wander."

Cinderella was about to become what she'd said she'd been, to experience the unpleasantries she claimed to have already experienced. Interesting, I thought as I sipped the drink that tasted of peach and green flashes. Painfully ironic.

"I believe we are what we decide to be," she said. She paced back and forth along the side of the terrace. She apparently had no fear of tumbling over, although the wall was barely as high as her ankle. Well, I thought, she's used to it up here. As for me, ordinary people like me never had the chance to sit in the sky this way. I felt relaxed, comfortable and removed from all I had known in my prior life. For a moment, I wondered if there weren't a potion in my peach drink, but it seemed a silly idea, so I let it drift away along with the breeze coming off the far hills, the gentle sweep of the princess' gown as she paced back and forth and the quiet rumbles of the snoring servant.

"I believe that if you can imagine something, you can make it happen," Eleanora said. "I am what I believe I am, and I believe I am a royal Princess, the once and future Princess."

I closed my eyes and let her words roll over me, as I waited for the significant ones, the ones that would tell me how we were going to untangle our various messes. Anyway, I'd heard variations of this speech from her before. But of what use is New Age wisdom in a place where it's always the same age, always long ago and far away or once upon a time, a combination of then and now where new is nothing special.

"I cannot believe that I am destined to leave this behind, to be shamed by my family for harmless exaggerations that elevated all of our status by getting me this position."

I opened one eye at that, to see if she was, perhaps, joking. None of us at the bedraggled, besieged homestead had noticed any elevated status these past few years. But she wasn't kidding. Her expression was tense as she paced. She stopped only when she heard a blare of trumpets. "That means he's on his way," she said. "They do that sort of thing when either of us is about to appear. I find it quite satisfying." Then she resumed her pacing and whatever her monologue was. A plea? An explanation? An apology? I waited, only half listening.

Which is why I missed most of what preceded ". . . only solution I could figure out, and frankly, this will solve all my problems, all at once." I opened both eyes wide. It was supposed to be *our* problems we were solving, wasn't it? Was this going to be the diamond slippers all over again?

I only began to grasp what she meant and what was happening after I heard another blare of trumpets, saw her look down and then in about three quick movements, roll forward one of the enormous planters that must have been on a platform and then, when it was at the edge, push, hard against the rim of the planter.

Those small motions from the buffed Princess were enough to tilt the planter off its platform.

"No!" I screamed as I ran to where she was. But it was too late. The clay and dirt and porcelain mass plummeted down, directly onto the royal head of Charming himself.

"Eleanora," I gasped. "You—on purpose, you—how could—"

At which point she screamed with all the force I remembered from her childhood tantrums. Screamed and screamed and screamed.

The pathetic servant girl awoke and leaped to her feet, rubbed at her eye and said "Your highness?" over and over.

"She killed him!" Eleanora screamed, pointing at me.

"Me? I tried to stop you from—"

Half the palace's underlings rushed up the stairs to the screaming princess. The other half were audible below, keening over of the late Prince Charming.

"She was jealous of us!" Cinderella screamed between

sobs. "Hated me! Consumed with bitterness because nobody wanted her. So she—look what she did to my Prince!"

Need we go into further detail? Do you think her subjects said, "We believe that your vile step-sister is telling the truth when she protests her innocence"?

Of course they didn't. As always, they believed their golden, shining princess, widowed at such a young and tragic age. They cherished her, protected her, made her absolute ruler until such time one of her sons would be ready, if either boy could ever pass their exams.

Of course the libel suit was forgotten. The remainder of the family was too terrified of the new Queen's power and wrath to do anything but leave quietly in the middle of the night, and I cannot blame them.

I couldn't leave with them, of course. Instead, I sit in this dungeon to which I am eternally condemned—Cinderella was lenient, granting me life instead of an instant beheading. I am supposed to be grateful as I grow to understand what "ever after" truly means.

But still, with some hope, I ask every set of eyes that peeks into my cell to listen to this story and try to right the wrongs that have befallen me. To see Cinderella for what she is and the me for what I am. I've asked them to test me—to find wizards or truth potions, to loose spirits who will determine the truth.

All they do is laugh at me. I'm a joke, an easy amusement for the bored. A one-woman sideshow. Jesters do imitations of me at court for after-dinner amusement.

Up there in all her splendor Cinderella is surrounded by adoring crowds, and down here with spiders and lizards for company, I continue as I have through the millennia, unhappily ever after. Still, I tell everyone the story.

Now I've told you. Try this version the next time your kids want a bit of Fairyland as a bedtime tale. Try truth.

Or do you still believe in Fairytales?

CLEAR SAILING

Mr. Hackett stood at the entrance to the terrace, straining to hear beyond the cocktail chatter and shush of the palm fronds, out to the ocean. It was music to him—the sound of silent power, stealth, deceptive surface calm. He listened, inhaled deeply and felt ready to take on the night.

The group of executives—his team, his people—were backlit by the sunset over the ocean. They looked elegant in their tropical finery ("resort casual" the agenda had suggested.) Dressed for success, even at play, with their wives as their most spectacular accessories.

As the company's annual profits rose, the annual retreats had been set at ever more opulent, spectacular and exotic resorts. As if to keep up with the scenery, the wives were likewise upgraded, becoming ever younger and more aesthetically pleasing.

A quick check by Mr. Hackett failed to reveal his own, unupgraded, wife, so, he decided, he was free to openly appreciate the flowerlike beauties as they posed, laughing excessively at whatever anyone said. Honing their wife-acts, Mrs. Hackett would say. She, the queen of fake-laughter, made fun of newcomers who copied her act. She didn't like the ingenues, as she called them, the ever-younger wives, and she nastily suggested that they were evidence of some failing on their husbands's part. Some childish belief that a spouse

171

could turn back the clock. "They confuse women and mirrors," she'd murmured—Hannah Hackett lacked the oomph to even raise even her voice—"as if what they see is their own reflection, their own youth. Their wives are their very own portraits of Dora Ann Gray."

He had no idea what she was talking about, except that it was more proof of her menopausal jealousy. He smiled with pleasure at the young women's animation, their overlarge gestures, their bright laughter. Their great legs. Their great tans. Their everything.

He was starved for such views. The sight of Mrs. Hackett across a patio, let alone a marital bed, had long since lost its charm. And his short-term changes of scene were no longer enough. Why should he have to sneak a few hours of pleasure? He was the boss. The Number One man. Look what his underlings had! It was time for a major revision of his landscape. He deserved it. He'd earned it.

Hannah Hackett had been a ball of fire when they met, but the sad truth was, she was down to cool embers now. Whatever had once been had melted into a lump, with all the beauty and interest lumps had. His wife, as they said, hadn't grown. Except in the hips. And waist. And thighs and upper arms. And her mind and interests were so narrowly focused on him, his career, his children, his home, he felt as if he were in a straitjacket.

The young women gazed adoringly at their men. They knew which side their bread was buttered. And their men's jowls almost jiggled with smug contentment, as well they might. They'd made it, and they had the wives to prove it.

A person of consequence attracted the best of breed. It was nature's way, survival of the fittest, nothing more, nothing less. Made the struggling and scrimping and clawing your way up worth while. To the victor goes the spoils.

Speaking of something spoiled, where was Hannah? The least she could do was be here, do her one and only job.

He frowned as a deafening buzz obliterated the sound of the ocean. A helicopter, he realized, circling the darkening sea. Jesus! Hannah was out sailing. Was she still out there, and in trouble? Sailing was Hannah's one remaining passion, if the word 'passion' could be applied to something basically dull. Hannah-like: quiet, solitary and interminable.

So she could be out there, in trouble . . . His mind raced around that possibility until he realized he'd seen her in the lobby an hour ago, back from the day's sail. The helicopters weren't searching for Hannah.

His regret was nothing like a twinge. It was more like a heart attack.

What was he going to do about that woman? He wanted her away. Permanently. Out of his sight. Didn't want to start a mess, but somehow . . . But actually, she'd probably be relieved to be retired from being the CEO's wife. Even phlegmatic Hannah must be bored with her do-nothing life.

Problem was, judges tended to be over-generous to long-term first wives who had no life or income of their own. He'd have to get the accountant on it immediately, move funds, take care of things before he said a word to Hannah.

It wasn't as if Hannah cared about him. If she did, she'd notice him, including noticing where he went, with whom he spent time. Wonder where he was when he wasn't home. But she had no idea, zero, about his extra-curricular activities. Didn't that mean she didn't care? That he was below her notice? That she had no interest in him? Given that, there was no reason for him to feel guilty when his own wife didn't notice and didn't mind his playing around.

He was tethered to the most overly-domesticated woman on God's green earth, and if it didn't have to do with recipes, child-rearing or gardening, she wasn't interested.

She did have a little stubborn streak, though. Might not leave quietly. It would be about money. His money. The woman had been an economics major, after all, and she knew things. All through their marriage, she'd invested and rolled-over and planted whatever portion of his income was possible in places where it was almost sure to grow. Even apart from stocks and real estate—even the art she'd selected—he'd definitely have to work on getting that all in his own name—had appreciated to the point where it was worth a small fortune. She had the touch. He just didn't want her touch in his wallet.

Besides, it was high time she did something for herself, quit the pro-wifing circuit. She should be grateful to him for terminating the marriage. Thank him for setting her free so she could finally find out what it was she'd rather do. Lord knows that once upon a time she muttered about lost options. Of course, he blamed that on the damned women's movement that had to come along during his marriage. No man in history had to listen to his wife demand "more" or "it all", whatever that meant. Why, then, all of a sudden, when it was Richard Hackett's turn, did everything have to change? But even that was long ago, and Hannah hadn't wanted anything since. He'd jog her memory, remind her about wanting more, wanting it all.

His reverie was interrupted by Susie Waters, the newest of the new crop of wives. She was smiling at him, but not with your basic cocktail hour smile, or the warm but respectful one given the boss. Susie was making major eye contact. Massaging him with her eyes.

Her husband Sam was talking to someone else about golf. The man should keep a better eye on his little woman. His job wasn't good enough, high up enough, to allow for an acting out wife. She was not an asset to the corporation.

As for being a private asset, one he might enjoy, well, that was different.

Besides, whatever happened was Hannah's fault. She should be here if she didn't want this to happen. In return for the easiest life on the planet, the very least she could do for him was show up when she was expected to. If ever he'd needed proof that Hannah was tired of this life and its duties, would be glad to be rid of it, this was it.

Setting her free would be doing her a favor.

He walked over to where Susie Waters was accepting a fresh martini from the waiter. She took a second one off the serving tray and held it out to him.

He accepted her offer. All her offers.

"You know, science has proven it is humanly possible for a person to survive twenty-four hours without talking to her mother," Jared Tomkins said.

Betsy Hackett Tomkins screwed her face into a mockpout. "Mom's the exception to the rule. Her family's her entire life. She'll be upset if I don't tell her right away."

"Is this worth interrupting her vacation? She's in the Caribbean, for God's sake. Tell her when she gets back."

Betsy shook her head with loving exasperation. "She isn't like us, hon," she said. "She doesn't have anything to interrupt. A vacation's from something. What would that mean to her? She's there because Daddy's there. She's Mrs. Richard Hackett here, and Mrs. Richard Hackett there. On the job. I feel sorry for her."

"She'd be Hannah Hackett if it didn't sound like a coughing disease," Jared said.

Betsy mock-scowled again and dialed the long-distance number her mother had left with her. Jared didn't really mind the call. He couldn't afford to. Her mother, whispering

"Don't tell Daddy. If he knew I was managing the money this well, he'd reduce my allowance!" had been astoundingly generous to the two of them and to all her children and grandchildren.

"Besides," Betsy said, covering the mouthpiece, "they'll be out for the evening, and I'll leave a message. Won't actually have to talk." The truth was, her mother had nothing to say, but said it at length.

The phone rang only once in the far-away hotel room before she heard her mother's eager, "Hello? Yes?"

"Mom! I'm—you okay?"

"Of course—who is—Betsy? What's wrong?"

"Nothing, Mom. It's just—what are you doing in your room at this hour?"

"Waiting for your call, obviously. What is it, darling? What's wrong?"

"Mom? Cara took her first step today."

"The dear! She didn't! But she's so young!"

"We were shocked, too."

"A prodigy. An athlete. She'll be an Olympic star."

Her mother always spun the simplest achievements into signs of stratospheric triumphs where her children and now, her grandchildren were concerned. Never, however, for herself. She was not an achiever beyond the kitchen.

A month earlier, at a conference—Betsy was a lawyer, working part-time on the Mommy-track with a large firm—she'd been introduced to a guest speaker, a Superior Court judge, who, it turned out, had gone to college with her mother. "And how is Hannah?" the woman had asked. "What's she running? We voted her most likely to be the first woman president. Haven't seen her name in the White House, so where is she?"

It was embarrassing answering that, no matter how many

euphemisms she used. Her mother wasn't running the world or running for office. Her mother was running a household. Housewife, plain and simple, emphasis on simple. "But she's the happiest person I know," Betsy had said in her defense, and unbelievable as it was, it seemed true. Hannah Hackett always seemed contented, although her daughter couldn't imagine why. Devoting your life and energies to a selfish, cold man didn't seem the world's most gratifying job. But for reasons unknown, her mother had settled down and hunkered in and never looked back or out.

"Excuse me? What's that?" Her mother's telephone chatter apparently required a response.

"I can barely hear myself thinking—there's a helicopter over the ocean. Wait, there's actually two—no, three of them. Searchlights on the water. Oh, dear."

"I'm glad you're safely back on shore," Betsy said.

"You worry too much! I had a lovely long sail today, and I expect to have an even lovelier, longer one tomorrow. The men will be playing golf for most of the day, so I am free of wifely duties and I can be out on the ocean forever. And I am a very, very cautious woman."

"Know what?" Betsy said, "it's probably not a rescue at all. It's a drug bust. To add a little excitement to your trip." She chuckled.

"Betsy! This is a respectable—Anyway, I'm late for cocktails. Daddy will be looking for me."

"I didn't mean to make you uncomfortable," Betsy said. "Sorry. I was joking because you get so uppity when we suggest water safety. So be careful, okay? The water looks calm, but things happen, as you can hear."

"Stop worrying. I'm an excellent sailor, and you know it. After all, Daddy trained me."

That wasn't true. Betsy's parents had taken lessons together, and Hannah had excelled, had been a natural. Betsy's father hated it, could never figure out which direction the wind came from. He wanted motors and noise and gave up on sailing almost instantly. But as always, Hannah deferred to her husband, insisted he was the best, asked him for help when none was needed. It wasn't worth mentioning. Hannah Hackett wore rose-colored blinders. Always had and always would.

After again marveling at the baby's amazing agility, mother and daughter promised to talk the next day and said good-night, with hugs and kisses to all and sundry.

"I'm sure they'll find the sailor," Betsy said by way of closing. "Don't worry, Mom, and be sure and wear your life jacket all day tomorrow."

"I always do," Hannah Hackett said. "Daddy would be upset otherwise."

Liz Evans was about to go stark raving mad listening to these insane, politicking, stupid women! She would have said you could rip her tongue out before she'd trash her sisters, but she didn't want these women as siblings! She wanted . . . wanted what she and her husband, David, were supposedly having. A vacation. Pina coladas and margaritas under the beach umbrellas. Romance, soft breezes. Tropical paradise. Dancing under the stars.

Not this. This was work. Except that she liked her work, and hated this.

Liz felt her chin push out, like a pouting child's until she realized it and realigned her face.

Ungrateful bitch, she told herself. Half the world's starving to death, living in hovels, and even most of the lucky ones are enduring winter, while you're in paradise, compliments of your husband's employer.

But she knew that wasn't true. A nice stage, yes, but she was working on it, performing in a play set in paradise. It was all an act—the setting, the lush room, the complimentary bathrobes and breakfasts and all her lines. Her gestures, her moves. Not even improv—all pre-scripted. This is how a junior executive's wife acts. This is what she wears. Drinks. Laughs at. Discusses. And worst of all, the play was a farce. Was Liz actually supposed to care about Mitzi's remodeling job and precisely how long and tedious her extravagances could be, let alone the exact shade of tile she picked for the guest bath after an agonizing, heart-breaking hunt? Did Liz need to care about how magnificent Violet's son had been as Hamlet in his ninth grade production of same? Thank God her corporate wifely duties hadn't included attending the show.

On the edge of the patio, Susie Waters' was ignoring the script, writing her own. Where had the woman left her brains? Maybe they were down in her cleavage, where her spandex dress had squeezed them to death.

In any case, Susie wasn't playing her part as written by Hannah Hackett, the perfect corporate wife.

The two women on the other side of Liz were doing their bit. Their jobs, like Liz's, were to look good, admire anyone who worked for the company, and to demonstrate the worth of the company's paychecks by becoming expert consumers. The two wives sounded in ecstasy because designer wear was less expensive on the island, and they breathlessly described every name-brand piece of attire they hoped to find the next day. "The Calvin Klein that—" floated across the terrace. "Manolo—" "Prada! . . ." ". . . tiny purse shaped like a peacock, that—"

Women were supposed to be part of the greater world now, not standing in separate clumps talking about kids and bathroom tile and how most efficiently to spend money somebody else earned. Women weren't supposed to be parlaying their bodies, climbing the corporate ladder via new mates. Women had evolved. At least half the women on this patio had jobs, but it was company policy to treat such activities as time-fillers, inconsequential and somewhat embarrassing hobbies.

Liz kept her daily activities almost a dirty secret at company events. She wanted to fit in for David's sake. Not that she could understand why a wife who wasn't a clone of the CEO's other half made a man unfit to construct engineering projects, but so it seemed. This was supposedly one big family and dad, the CEO himself, didn't like his female kids to be distracted by their own concerns.

So far, she and David were successfully faking compliance. David was the official whiz-kid, the youngest senior executive in the firm. Soon enough, he'd be able to either break from here or take it over. It was in her own interests to help him reach that goal. Play the game, no matter how she felt about it.

And, damn, there she was. Hannah Hackett, looking flushed. What on earth had penetrated the fogbank she lived inside. Hannah spent a whole lot of time out at sea, both figuratively and literally. "Mrs. G.," Liz said warmly. "You look like you got some sun today. Your cheeks are pink."

Hannah put a fingertip to her face, as if testing its color in Braille. "I was out for a long time, but I thought I used enough sunblock, but . . . you know, I'm just excited, is all."

"About the drug bust?" a red-haired woman asked.

Mrs. Hackett looked confused. "The what?"

"Didn't you hear it? Helicopters all over the ocean. A policeman told me they were tipped off that smugglers were dropping drugs off this beach, this hotel."

"For heaven's sake—my daughter made a joke and I—but—are you saying they're doing this now? While we're here?" Mrs. Hackett said.

The woman could be amusing, Liz decided. The dimwit thought Colombian drug dealers should check Hannah Hackett's travel plans before making their own.

"The policeman said the beach might be closed tomorrow if it isn't all wrapped up tonight."

The red-head shivered. "He had this enormous gun or rifle or bazooka, I don't know what it was, but I wasn't about to protest!"

"But since it's news to you, Mrs. H., that obviously wasn't what had you excited," another gushing middle-management wife said. "So what was it?"

Hannah Hackett smiled. "You'll think it silly after news of a drug bust, but my daughter phoned to say our youngest grandchild just took her first step."

Liz smiled, as if that were the biggest news she'd heard in years. The other women cooed and ahhed. Astounding that a human child had decided to walk.

Another five minutes of this and she'd run screaming into the sea. Helicopters or no helicopters.

The hypocrites asked if Hannah had any photos, knowing full well that Hannah always carried gigantic handbags, bags large enough to contain a bulging photo album. "This is Jason in his kindergarten Halloween parade. He was dressed as a clown, isn't that dear? I just love old-fashioned costumes. Actually, I sewed it up for him. Such fun! And this is Terry when he lost those teeth—"

"Haven't they grown, though," the women murmured. As if that were surprising.

"Looks like he's going to be a basketball player!"

Liz knew she ought to come up with her own inanity, but

her mind was blank, which in turn produced panic. Your mind wasn't allowed to go blank until you were the CEO's wife. Until you were Hannah Hackett.

Which meant, perhaps, that it was an inevitable transition, which was terrifying in itself because Liz had noticed a Phi Beta Kappa key on Hannah Hackett's charm bracelet. "Oh, that," Hannah had said when Liz commented. "That was long ago. You know, I earned my M.R.S. degree and that was that. Not that I'm saying it was a waste. Not at all. My major, economics, has helped me be a better wife, better at managing a household." And then she laughed, dismissing her past achievements, dismissing herself.

"But don't you—did you—do you ever think about—" Liz was a partner in a landscape design firm. If David said she had to give it up—well, that was unthinkable. He wouldn't, and if he did for some sick reason, she'd refuse.

"We decided that one career was all this family could handle, and I agreed," Hannah had said, not noticing her own words. *We* decided, but then *she* agreed? Who was the "we" then? Liz was sure that was the way Richard Hackett practiced domestic democracy. He was the majority, and that was that.

"You know, we moved seven times," Hannah had continued. "How could I have any kind of job? Moving, plus taking care of the house and the family, and doing it right was my job and it was more than full-time."

Liz understood this as a warning and polite rebuke, but something in her insisted on following the thought through. "Even now that the children are grown-up and you're in one place?" she asked. She smiled, as if all this talk was inconsequential chit-chat, not at all disapproving, not at all real.

"Who has the time?" Hannah asked lightly, all wide-eyed innocence. "My calendar's full between the household maintenance, our social obligations, the grandchildren, the dogs and volunteering for the Foundation."

Ah, the Foundation. Second only to the grandchildren as a topic of staggeringly boring conversation. Not that it wasn't worthy—just achingly uninteresting. Trust Hannah to have found The Shadow Foundation, a hands-on, unglamorous aggregate, Liz assumed, of professional Mommies like Hannah who volunteered their time cooking and reading and sewing and tutoring. Extremely worthy, extremely dull listening. Very Hannah.

"Several years ago, I committed to provide three dozen apple pies a month," Hannah said. "Two for the homeless outreach program, and one for the women's shelter. That's a lot of baking, but how could I give it up? I hope I don't sound like I'm bragging but I've been told my apple pie is their most popular dessert. They've put my recipe in the volunteer newsletter this month. I didn't want my name involved, so I asked them to call it "A Nonna's Apple Pie." Nonna's Italian for grandmother, did you know that? I like how it sounded—almost like 'anonymous', get it? I'm not Italian and neither is apple pie, so it makes it funnier, I think. Maybe now, with the recipe in print, maybe some other people will help with the baking. Which would give me more time for the grandchildren."

Liz gave up. Anonymous's apple pies, which Liz had to admit were exceptional, went out in miniature versions in homemade Christmas baskets to all employees each year. Plus tiny tarts, miniature loaves of tea breads and intricately designed and decorated cookies. Liz was grateful for small mercies—Hannah didn't weave the baskets herself.

Liz watched as Hannah's glance floated toward the edge of the patio, where Susie Waters and Richard Hackett appeared to be having an intense conversation. Except that Liz had spoken with Susie long enough to know that the woman couldn't spell conversation, let alone make it. But whatever the words were that passed between the two of them, Susie Waters and Richard Hackett's body language was as easy to read as if it had Supertitles translating it in enormous print.

Hannah's glance floated on without pause, as if all she'd seen was another piece of the landscape. She was one oblivious woman. You could hardly blame Richard Hackett for seeking stimulation elsewhere, although the sort of stimulation Susie Waters could provide was not what Liz meant. But even a woman as dull as Hannah should feel a spark of indignation. Or maybe Susie was welcome—a relief shift to take care of an onerous wifely duty and give Hannah more time for baking for the homeless and playing with her grandchildren.

Liz's husband flashed her a private smile that heated the air between them, and she remembered again why she was here and why it was worth playing her role. As long as she knew he was playing along with her, that they were a team and that both of them recognized the game for all it could yield and what it was, then this was a beautiful island and life was fine.

Liz turned her own smile on Hannah, with honest gratitude. She was glad to have been presented with this woman early on as an example of everything to be avoided. A woman who had devoted all her talents to fostering her ungrateful, philandering, negligent husband's career, a woman without an interest of her own—except for sailing, and how often did she get to do that, except on corporate getaways?—a woman whose entire life revolved around others.

I will never give up my own identity the way you have, Liz silently vowed. I will never be completely dependent on my husband's earnings and my husband's pleasure in me. I will never let my interests and life and ambitions be squeezed away by meaningless corporate pleasures. Thank you Saint Hannah, for showing me precisely how not to be.

"I am so very sorry, Madam," the man in white said.

"Excuse me?" The woman stopped sharply, as if he'd accosted her. She stood stark still, seemingly confused and overburdened, her flowered dufflebag clutched to her chest. "I was just going to—"

"But you see, the Marina is closed," the man said.

"It can't be—I have a boat reserved."

He shook his head. There were notices posted every five feet. Stupid Americans can't read. Won't. Kings of the world. Rules didn't apply to them. Signs didn't apply to them. First, the bikini girlies who didn't care what the signs said, they wanted their time on the sand. This precise stretch of sand, because it was near their overpriced rooms. But this dowdy one wasn't a bikini girlie, for sure. Dressed in baggy pants and shirt, clutching her enormous pink flowered old-lady bag. But not old enough to be this confused, and if she was this easily muddled, if she ignored signs this much, she shouldn't be thinking of sailing out there by herself.

"I took a boat out yesterday, too," she added as if she'd read his mind. "Right here. From this very spot."

"Yes, Madam. We're so very sorry for the inconvenience, but it is forbidden for you to go on this beach today. However, there is—"

"But we—my husband's company—this is our annual—our people are entitled to all the amenities of this—"

"Madam, please. There are police all over this beach, and they're armed. You don't want to be shot, do you?"

"*Shot?* This is a resort, not a . . . why on earth would anybody shoot me? I wouldn't even be on the beach. I'd be sailing. And why are those policemen out there now? This is a terrible time to have a practice drill."

"Madam, this is real. The authorities believe that drug smugglers have targeted this beach as a rendezvous point where they transport the stuff. A drop-off."

"I heard that last night—but that was last night!"

"Yes, Madam. And this is the morning. And they are still not yet here."

"And they won't be. In broad daylight? At a resort? That's ridiculous!"

"That's all I know. Hide in clear sight, maybe. I'm only a security guard working with the police to protect you." Goddamn rich bitch thinks she owns the island, owns me. He couldn't stand how he had to smile and keep the polite patter up while she tells him her people have these rights on *his* island.

"Now you listen here," she said. "This foolishness is making me waste a perfectly beautiful morning. I'd like to register a complaint. Not against you: you're just doing your job. If my husband had known such things happened here, we would have never—"

"Yes, Madam. This is very unusual, I assure you. But it is also very regretful." Go ahead. Complain because our crystal ball didn't work, so we didn't know when something was going to happen for the first time. Complain as if drug smugglers have schedules, predictable drop-off points, the way trains do. And because it's your ocean. You're paying for it, drug drop or not. "Best talk to the person at the main desk," he said.

She sighed, and then she nodded, the way maybe a queen would, and huffed off.

And here came another one with her rear hanging out in a thong, and her chest barely covered at all. And all of it inside a transparent so-called jacket. He stood straighter, smoothed his moustache and smiled. "Beach is closed today, Madam," he said. "We have transportation to the neighboring beach just beyond the jetty, however, if you will go up to the main house."

She looked startled, then pouty, then she shrugged and agreed. Good. He got to watch that thonged backside all the way up the hill to the main house.

She couldn't believe how easy it was. Every time. Like blowing magic powder in everybody's eyes, making them see only what you wanted them to see.

The breeze fluttered Hannah Hackett's hair. She lay back, her head cushioned by her pink flowered beach bag as she sunbathed in the late afternoon heat, eyes closed in a blissful half-daze. Arturo the sailor was as excellent as was Arturo the lover. She let her mind drift back to the past several hours alone with him, in a private, hidden cove. Lovely. She was still slightly breathless. Arturo did everything brilliantly.

Even bake apple pies. Three dozen of them at a clip. And how their scent filled the house while the two of them filled the baking time.

She was free. Nobody would connect Hannah Hackett, Richard's wife, fuddy-duddy complainer at the resort's beach, with the lady who'd hired a man to sail her out of a marina halfway across the island.

Let Arturo steer the boat. Let him run the business from now on. She trusted him at the helm of anything, and she didn't need to be captain of anything anymore. She was happily retiring.

There was nothing like the sea, and nothing like making sure that the island's woefully inadequate police force would be massed elsewhere. She'd done this before, on other islands and on the coasts of several small countries. That's what set her operation apart. She wasn't as greedy as her competitors, many of whom were now either dead or in some country's jails. But marriage and motherhood teaches many valuable lessons—how to make sacrifices, to defer and distract, and give a little up. She transferred those skills to her business and sacrificed a part of the whole. A small part.

That set them apart. That diverted the local constables. That avoided notice. That, and the fact they used sailboats midway, had no set routes, no set country, no pattern any official body could fathom. Everything depended on where Mr. Hackett's boondoggle business trips took them. Once she knew the next destination, she and Arturo worked out the logistics, part of which was sacrificing a bit of the haul to put the police on alert at the wrong place, waiting for the rest of the drop to float in while she and Arturo carried on business—and carried on—elsewhere. From their first job on, the idea worked, and it was all, always, clear sailing ahead.

She wasn't the sort to arouse suspicions. For all the years she'd run her business from exotic ports of call taking major risks, using ever-changing ruses and plans—all anybody saw was a dithering, boring middle-aged woman. Their radar was shut down, their suspicions nonexistent. At Customs, too. Not once since her first hot-flash had she been stopped or inspected. She was that most respectable and least-feared of creatures—a middle-aged, middle-class woman. They waved her through.

At first it had annoyed her. She felt stripped of her power as a woman. But then she realized she could use her invisibility to her advantage, amass power through the gift of not mattering.

"You seem quiet today, my love," Arturo said. "Are you sad about giving up the business?"

"Not at all," she said. "It's time. It's your turn. And it's not like I'm giving up you."

He smiled and blew her a kiss. She wondered how long they'd last as lovers once she was no longer Captain. Days? Weeks? Well, for however long. He'd set the stage for his departure by turning over the apple-pie duties to a small bakery that promised to follow his recipe. She'd known it was a gallant, quiet, first step out the door. But it had been splendid for a long time now, and all things change and move on. He'd been a particularly apt and willing learner, and not only about business. He was an elegant man, and she'd miss him.

But with or without him, she was going to enjoy every second of her retirement. Except, maybe, for one detail giving her minor qualms. "I'm a little sorry about Richard," she murmured.

"Why waste emotion on such a rude man?"

Arturo was correct. She gave up the qualm and decided to enjoy that aspect of her impending retirement, too. Richard lacked manners, flaunting his flirtation with that set of mammary glands. Right there, in front of everybody, including the glands' husband. What was he implying—that CEO's had droit de seigneur? That executives got to sleep with whomever was attached to somebody lower on the organizational chart?

Power hadn't set well with Richard. He'd been in decline since his first promotion and this shameless, public display was the final straw. She'd declared their marriage contract null and void. Until last night, she hadn't been positive about eliminating Richard, but enough was enough. He'd embarrassed her.

Besides, the fact that he'd been so blatant about it meant that he was planning to end the marriage. Too bad and very stupid of him. She couldn't wait to see how it was when they returned home. He'd be on the phone to his accountant—if he hadn't already been—planning to move funds and hide assets. She'd make sure he lived long enough to discover that the money had already been juggled out of sight. And the art. Everything.

Not that she'd needed any of it. She simply wanted to make a point, make him understand her powers, at least a little. As for funds, she was incredibly wealthy, enough of the money carefully laundered by virtue of it's supposedly being his money. A perk of being a corporate wife. She had more than enough for herself, for her children and all the others through her Shadow Foundation. She'd named it in honor of herself, of how effectively she was ignored at home and out-side. Like that radio show she'd heard as a child, about a man who became invisible, but still saw the evil that men did. Through her foundation, she funded direct assistance pro-grams for whatever bothered her in the way people treated other people. The Foundation, on whose board she sat—nominated because of her husband's position—was run by people who had no idea of its hidden and complex origins. But she'd made sure it was run the way she wanted it to be, and she'd sufficiently endowed it that it could carry on without additional funds, so she'd be retiring from that, too.

Initially, Hannah had moral qualms about running a drug cartel, but given that all the money went for the greater good, she felt she was funneling these profits away from worse hands. Aside from the trusts for her grandchildren and other people who never suspected who their benefactor was, and the art, and the real estate, much of which she rented out to deserving people at below-market rates, and the Foundation, she'd invested a great deal of the enormous revenues in start-up businesses, under the banner of Nonnamus Venture Capital. She liked the play on 'Nonna', the grandma, and everybody (except businessmen, apparently) knew that Anonymous was a woman.

Via Nonnamus, the drug money was doing good both for the fledgling companies and for her. Her choices had been sound. A woman had to take care of herself.

It had all worked according to plan. Except for the Richard part. Pity, but he'd forced her hand. Luckily, her business was full of people who knew how to take care of such problems.

Besides, with Richard dead, she'd also be retiring from that most onerous of jobs, Being Hannah Hackett, the woman stupid enough to be married to such a wretch of a man. Such a relief to drop that act, shed that skin, come out of the Mrs. CEO closet! Never to drag photo albums of her grandchildren again. Never to carry pink flowered bags. Always to talk about interesting things, or to remain silent, or walk away from bores.

"You're right," Hannah now said to Arturo. "Richard is a rude man."

Arturo nodded. The skin on his back was tanned to the color of cherrywood. "It is regrettable, but we must attend to the problem of your husband. When do you think?"

"How about the first time he has an assignation with Miss Breast?" Hannah asked. "On the way to the love nest." She'd long known the address of his pied a terre, the value of its furnishings, as well as the names of everyone who visited there with him. Nonnamus Real Estate owned the building. She enjoyed secretly being Richard's landlady, and she made sure he paid top dollar.

"On the way there?" Arturo asked. "Not even letting him satisfy his lust one last time?"

She shrugged. "Given the number of times he's already

satisfied his lust in that apartment, and given how very rude he was last night—"

"He has had his quota? Enough is enough?"

"More efficient this way. And make sure it's both of them."

"The girl-woman, too?"

The addition of Susie had been spontaneous, but Hannah was a woman who was used to thinking on her feet and she trusted her instincts "Why not?" she said. "Make it a twofer. Nobody will mourn either one of that set of boobs."

Arturo laughed at her pun. His English was as finely honed as all his other talents.

She lay in the sun, her head resting on a pink flowered dufflebag filled with photos of her grandchildren and several dozen million dollars worth of merchandise, her body still imprinted by Arturo's.

Life was good indeed. The future, rich and unburdened, glimmered atop the sea's shining face. Clear sailing ahead.

HEART BREAK

"Emma," Vivian Carter said, "I was thinking . . ." She lapsed off into dreamy silence, but through the years, Emma had come to expect these pauses. Vivian's thoughts meandered through private byways. Eventually, and at her own pace, she'd get back to whatever was on her mind.

Emma Howe was in no hurry. She was enjoying both her beer and the quiet. She'd tolerated Vivian's unfinished sentences for over two dozen years, amazing herself, because she wasn't excessively tolerant of anything, she'd been informed more than once, and Vivian's brain too often seemed covered with bubble wrap.

But this was a day for savoring Vivian-provided time lags, for remembering the point of living in California. After the endless battering of an El Nino winter, the air was scrubbed to a high polish as its light ricocheted off the bay onto every clearly etched object. She sat in the warm midst of the equivalent of an ice storm, only here, light coated each leaf and blade, light made the colors seem from a child's crayon box, and it extended across the bay to where San Francisco glittered, each building edged and highlighted with light.

On the north side of the bay, Emma sat at a table in an outdoor restaurant backed up to a hillside filled with long-stemmed matijila poppies. They looked blatantly false with their oversized white crinkled petals and bright yellow centers.

Emma felt a knotted portion of her innards relax. Vivian's invitation had come at just the right time. That morning, George, generally the most agreeable of men, had pushed her as close to a declaration of war as an unmarried, uncohabitating middle-aged woman felt willing to endure before calling it quits.

It had been ridiculous. All she'd done is be annoyed—with good cause—at her daughter, the oldest infant in the universe. "She's a whiner, nothing more and nothing less," she'd said. "Won't make up her mind or take responsibility and do something. It lets her get away with murder."

And blam, like that, George was on her case, accusing her, the most realistic of women, of seeing everything in black and white. "No greys!" he'd said, like an angry teacher flunking her for bad behavior. "You refuse to admit there's even such a color!"

That was nothing short of ridiculous. Emma was a private investigator. Her entire profession dealt with greys and the need to clarify and see through them. She knew grey. She just didn't like it. Didn't approve of it. Avoided it at all costs. Grey was dirt and fog and weariness. Grey was to get rid of.

Who could say what had set George off? Maybe he had hormonal problems. Male menopause or something as yet undiscovered.

Besides, when you got down to it, there *were* such things as right and wrong, and whining vacillation was on the column in Emma's ledger headed "wrong." Why should Emma change her views? They made sense. They organized the world, provided guidance.

And even if she spent her days plodding around on behalf of lawyers attempting to bend the law in their client's direction, that still was on the side of right. That was the law. Emma was against what was *wrong,* and she'd be damned before she'd apologize for keeping a clear head.

She tilted her face toward the sun like a creature just released from hibernation, pushing away the memory of George's disapproval.

"You aren't the Deity, Emma Howe." He'd said it softly, but the words made her want to order him out of her house. "You aren't God and you don't *know* everything and everybody the way you sometimes think you do. Bend a little. Give a little more. You want every problem solved, every mystery answered. Some things just don't have ready answers."

She never claimed omniscience, but dammit, Emma was a good judge of people. Had to be to survive. The only seriously wrong call she'd made was with her late and unlamented husband, Harry, but she'd been young and in lust back then. And Harry, incessantly providing proof of how bad her judgement had been, had taught her to be more discerning about people. So what the hell was George talking about?

George was a good man. He must have gotten out of her bed on the wrong side. Luckily, the phone had rung at precisely the necessary moment, and Vivian's invitation saved the rest of the day from degenerating into grey. Into wrongness.

Instead, it was Technicolor. Life was good, indeed. Good to have a Saturday to herself, out of the office, away from insurance cheats (bad) and missing teenagers (all pains in the butt were bad by definition) and sullen, reluctant witnesses (bad. Period.)

Don't try to tell her there were no absolutes. Maybe for parameciums there weren't, but humans with functioning brains knew right from wrong.

"I like that those are native plants," Vivian said, gazing

toward the stand of matijila poppies. "I like that nobody invented or imported them. They planted themselves. They're real, and as intended. I love it that something that extravagant just pops out of the earth on its own. And that they look fake, like the crepe paper flowers we used to make to decorate the gym for dances."

And that was part of why Emma accepted Vivian's soft-sided mind. No other woman she knew would follow "I've been thinking" with a metaphysical appreciation of native flora. She nodded her understanding. (She *did* know people, no matter what George said. You could. You had to, in fact. That didn't mean you thought you were God.) "Those poppies are so overstated, they're horticultural Tchaikovsky," Emma said with a smile.

Vivian looked startled, momentarily confused, then smiled. "Oh, my God, I'd forgotten that." She nodded and sipped wine before speaking again. "I must have sounded like such an idiot. All that blather about life as a grand symphony. Oh, what I wanted out of poor old life!"

They'd been so young, embarking on marriage, speculating about how it would be, planning—now there was a laughable thought—the rest of their lives. Emma's own marriage had ended at the Tawdry-R-Us motel off the freeway, her husband's heart overwhelmed on yet another of its side trips into adultery. "Dead of a half-night stand" was the epitaph for Harry and their future.

But Vivian's unrealistic, impossible marriage that seemed so removed from the real world that it was doomed, endured. The picture was fresh and vivid in Emma's mind. Vivian, dressed all in black so the world would know she was a genuine artist, declaiming for a life that was "pure Tchaikovsky—oversized, passionate, nothing ordinary or bland. Ever."

Her words had been emblazoned in Emma's memory

because—she said—she couldn't believe her ears, couldn't believe her friend was that hopelessly immature. The girl was marrying a medical student whose every drudgy nanosecond was devoted to his studies, his rounds, his patients, his future, and, in truth, to stunned self-wonderment. He was a good man, a dedicated man, but his first love was himself. Yet Vivian, whose two jobs would support them, saw them in a perpetual wild waltz, when everyone with normal vision knew she was going to barely see him at all for years. And when she did, they'd both be too tired to even dream about romantic excesses and their conversation was guaranteed to be about medical procedures.

But that wasn't the only reason Emma had remembered Vivian's words. They were etched on her braincells because she'd secretly envied anyone who could think in those terms, whose imagination was large enough, unself-conscious enough to consider such an idea, whose cellular material wasn't made of one hundred percent washable, durable, unbreakable fabric.

"But look," Emma said. "Here we are in what is laughingly called middle age although that assumes we'll live to be one hundred and ten—and you and Gene are still going strong, whatever the background music has become. You weren't a fool at all."

Vivian held her wine glass below her nose, as if sampling its bouquet. Her eyes were half lowered, her expression unreadable. "You're more or less the law," she finally said.

"Come again?" What road had led Vivian from poppy-admiration through Tchaikovsky to Emma's relationship to the law?

"Cops are the law," Emma said. "The law's the law, so lawyers are the law. But I'm . . . auxiliary law, at best. What made you say that?"

"I need to know." She sighed as she ran her finger around the wine glass.

Normally, at such a juncture, Emma made it clear that she didn't have all day. But as it happened, she did. And she was with Vivian, whose clock was set to a different measure than the seconds and minutes the rest of the universe used.

"If I tell you something," Vivian said, "something terrible, do you have to report it? Or do you have to keep it a secret like lawyers and priests do?"

"A confession?" Emma asked, smiling. Vivian, unsmiling, nodded.

If Vivian Carter confessed to anything more serious than sampling unpaid-for grapes at the supermarket, Emma would go home and tell George he was absolutely right. That she didn't know squat about anybody.

Vivian was the gentlest of women. Not that she didn't deal with her portion of the real world. In fact, she nurtured it. She was an art therapist at a center for emotionally disturbed children, and was outstanding at quietly finding a way into a child's locked up world. A year ago, Emma and George had gone to an event honoring Vivian. They'd sat with her husband, Gene, who never had acquired that haunted Tchaikovsky patina. Not in attitude and surely not in appearance. He looked wholesome and sturdy, scrubbed clean and trustworthy. He looked the way a cardiologist should look, like someone you'd trust with your heart. His faith in himself had been justified by time as he won awards and an international reputation. But that night, he'd stared with open adoration at his wife as she was praised from the podium. He seemed completely contented to bask in his wife's reflected glory. They'd all grown up and learned new, less troublesome music. Nobody wanted Tschaikovsky making life and death decisions about them. You wanted somebody like Gene.

Vivian treated her husband like a beloved artifact, cushioning him in a home decorated in the same soft and glowing colors she painted onto her canvases. She raised three fine children without seeming to raise her voice. She was generous to a fault, and slow to anger.

All of which would have long-ago put Vivian over the top of airy-fairiness and off Emma's list of acquaintances were all the sweetness and light not tempered by dollops of earthiness, good humor, intense honesty, surprising pragmatism, and talent. Vivian's paintings fascinated Emma, because they made it obvious that the woman, who lived only a few miles from Emma, inhabited an alternate universe with its own sky, earth and bay.

None of which could account for the troubled dark in Vivian's amber eyes, a shadow that wasn't part of her usual hesitations and conversational wanderings. Emma stifled her urge to smile. "How terrible?" she asked.

"You didn't answer. Would you have to tell? Could you keep this confidential?"

"You're worrying me," Emma said. "What are we talking about here?" What would the queen of pastel see as "terrible?"

Cruelty, Emma thought. Any variety. A prank turned sour. Elder abuse. She probably suspected somebody—a relative, a frail and elderly neighbor—was being neglected, or more actively abused. It would be like Vivian to notice—and like her to agonize over what to do. That was fine. At least she asked for advice, and Emma loved giving it. Loved being She Who Knows And Never Dithers.

"We're talking about murder," Vivian said.

Emma pulled back in her chair as if to avoid the suddenly hard-edge light. "I'm a P.I.," she said quietly. "It's only on TV that P.I.'s meddle in police investigations. I'd lose my license, even if I had a taste for that sort of thing."

"You wouldn't be meddling into anything," she said softly. "There is no investigation."

"If you have information about a murder that the police don't know about, you have to tell them, Viv."

"I can't."

"Then tell me and I'll tell them."

"They won't know what you're talking about." Vivian was almost inaudible.

"But you said—"

"It is murder," Vivian said more emphatically. "A kind of murder."

Emma relaxed. Not exactly murder, but a kind of murder. Of the spirit? The will? She'd been right in her initial assessment. This was Vivian and her "murder" wasn't the kind the law minds. Emma listened with tolerant amusement, waiting for what trivial mini-drama Vivian would present.

"Can I tell you? And then you can tell me what to do. You're always so sure of yourself, Emma. I get mired down, but you always—I so admire that about you."

Emma was delighted to have someone acknowledge what wasn't a fault, no matter what George thought, but a talent. Vivian seemed about to speak, but waitperson Jenny, who so introduced herself as she materialized at the table, needed to take their orders. Truth was, no matter what George had said, real life wasn't gray. There were two options in this life, the right and the wrong. Imagine the Ten Commandments according to George. "Maybe thou should . . ." "Sometimes thou shalt . . ." World was bad enough off with absolutes, but muddle things more with ifs and perhaps . . .

Furthermore, even Vivian, who might appear a ditz, knew what to do. People always did. They just wanted people like Emma around to insist they follow that right impulse. Emma was a professional prod, that was all.

Waitperson Jenny—Emma wanted to know why she had to know the name of someone she'd have a five minute relationship with—chirped the list of specials—exotic foodstuffs that hadn't existed when Emma was young. Emma ordered a cheeseburger, rare, and got a savage pleasure out of the waitress's barely controlled disapproval. Vivian ordered a concoction of various forms of plant life. And another glass of wine.

"Begin," Emma said the moment Jenny bounced off.

"If I only knew where . . ." Vivian said.

"At the beginning. Then go all the way through to the end." Fat chance having that be true with Vivian, but it never hurt to hope . All the same, Emma felt mild apprehension. Why wouldn't Vivian know where to begin?

"The beginning . . . maybe it was the Tchaikovsky life, maybe that was it. I had such high hopes. Correction. They were more than hopes. They were convictions. A credo. Gene was so . . . electrical. More alive than other men. I can be a little, um, less than directed. He seemed so *passionate* compared to me. I thought we were a cosmic combination."

This "murder" was about her marriage?

"So did Gene. He wanted that bigger and better life just as much as I did. He wanted to feel things to his toes, to never live dully. We were alike in that."

He had an affair, Emma assumed. Or is having one. Their marriage was being murdered. Kind of. But first, the story of how wonderful it once was. Even women hiring her to spy on their wandering mates began with the story of how it once had been. Even they, buying her services in a cut and dried transaction, had to offer up the sad trajectory of their love, to explain why they weren't run of the mill, but tragic figures worthy of attention. Over the years, over how many tables and desks, lunches, dinners, and drinks had she listened to women recite this litany? And sometimes, she'd been the one telling the tale.

"Gene got a lot of the adventure he wanted through his work. Through the instruments he's devised, the awards. In the world he chose, he's made it. The Eighteen-Twelve Triumphal music is playing all the time in his background." She smiled, half proudly, half wistfully.

"But real life wasn't what I'd imagined, Emma. For a long time, the work—mine and his during medical school and residency—and then the children—we were too busy to be Tchaikovsky. We were too busy treading water. I stopped painting, stopped all the art. Couldn't set up, couldn't afford sitters, couldn't find the time or even clear my mind long enough to see anything beyond the day itself. And then one day, I woke up and realized I was everything I hadn't wanted. I was ordinary as mud."

Emma's mind had wandered back to the days Vivian was remembering. Kids today—her own daughter Caroline—had no idea what a different world it had been back then. Women like Vivian, sick for personal expression, were told they were maladjusted. Didn't like being female. "Hardly ordinary," Emma said. "Everybody's marriage was crumbling in those days. Everybody's except yours. And you must remember that you were painting, at least a little, and definitely well, because I remember an exhibit where you won first prize."

After half a dozen years and two children with Harry Howe, his inability to hold a job plus his talent for gambling away whatever he'd managed to earn, Emma realized her life was not going to follow her carefully designed plan. The only jobs she could find for the longest time were poorly paid, menial foot-weary work that never advanced her life, just sustained it. She hadn't been to college, had no special skills.

Just debts. So the winter of that painting award Emma watched Vivian's life flower with her growing family, their new economic stability, her art, his medicine. Emma watched Vivian the dizzy one manage to have it all. And she tried not to envy, not to let the chilling grasp of jealousy ruin the relationship.

"That painting," Vivian murmured. "I didn't say it then, felt as if I was cheating, but that was an old painting. I'd done it years before the show. So don't, Emma," she said softly, brushing imaginary crumbs off the table. "Don't try to console or reassure me. That's your view of my life. I'm trying to tell you how it actually was. I wasn't unhappy—but I wasn't happy, either." She looked up and stopped speaking as Jenny put Emma's hamburger down as if it were contaminated, then beamed at Vivian as she reverently placed the sprouty offering in front of her.

"I was ashamed of myself, too," Vivian said as soon as Jenny turned her back. "Here I was with everything I could want, and more, and I felt half-dead. Numb inside. So I went for help."

Of course she would. Nobody opted to just plain get over it. Grow up. That had been part of the heated discussion with George this morning. Caroline had been contaminated growing up in Marin where there was a therapist on every street corner, and an ordinance against experiencing even a moment's pain. You lived at the end of the rainbow and you'd better enjoy it. Caroline had spent half her life and most of her money on cure-alls ever since, and nothing at all was cured.

George considered her opinion narrow-minded. They were going to have to, as they said in these parts, work on that. But for now, she kept her mouth shut. Vivian had gone for help. Emma would now undoubtedly endure second-hand revelations and insights and know that the help hadn't worked. You could see its failure in Vivian's desperately unhappy expression.

"I fell in love with my therapist," Vivian said. "I know how that sounds. I know it's a cliché, and I knew it then. But I also knew, almost immediately, he was the perfect person in the world for me."

Emma waited.

"We had an affair."

Damn whoever it was. That was a terrible thing—but not the way Vivian probably meant. To take advantage of a client's vulnerability was disgusting, and she was glad of the chance to tell Vivian so. No need to debate this one. Take the bastard to court. Rip up his license. "Okay, Vivian, you asked me what to do, and I'll tell you. Take him to—"

"We didn't have the affair while I was his patient. I stopped therapy—he suggested it. Months went by before . . ." She looked up. "Nothing was rushed into. I was married and so was he. But eventually . . . it lasted a year and a half. Well, there you have it."

No. She didn't. That was the terrible thing? The so-called murder? "When was this?"

"Fifteen years ago."

For God's sake but it had taken Vivian long enough to decide this was a big moral issue. "You don't need my opinion about that. Besides, it's over."

Vivian shook her head and lifted her wine glass again, drinking from it almost as if it were water. Emma ate hamburger. It seemed the wrong choice of food while listening to a tale of passion, somehow tactless, but all the same, she thoroughly savored it during the pauses Vivian's stuttering memory provided.

"It ended because it was wrong," Vivian finally said. "Too

hurtful. I was ready to leave my marriage, but he wouldn't do the same. There were good reasons. His wife wasn't well, and . . . in any case, it became too emotionally painful to continue. And I hated lying. Hated it. I decided to make my marriage work instead, to find my own way, get on with it. Gene and I saw a counselor together and talked things through, and . . ."

"He knew, then?"

She nodded. "I wanted the air clear between us. He was shocked, he was miserable, he was angry, he was depressed. He was all the things I guess people are. He was almost— pretty much—that passionate, crazy, over the edge man I'd thought I wanted. But I'd grown up, you see. It was awful. Most of all, he hated that I couldn't lie and say I'd never loved the other man. He wanted that to be the truth, but it wasn't. And he wanted me to hate the other man now that it was over, but I didn't. Why would I? He was loveable. He hadn't done anything to change that perception. I knew I'd love him till I died, although of course, I didn't say that to Gene. But I didn't say the words he was aching to hear, either. I didn't lie. It was bad enough that I'd cheated and lied for a year and a half. Gene's such a . . . *rational* man, a problem solver, a healer. But then, he talked about revenge, getting back— useless, meaningless, insane things like that. Completely unlike himself. Which is when, and why I realized I wanted him to be completely like himself. I wanted that calm intensity, and steadiness. And I'd ruined it, I thought. Smashed it. Except eventually, the rage and depressions passed, and the past began to feel like a disease we'd both recovered from. Life's been good ever since." She exhaled, as if after long exertion, and poked at her grassy salad. She looked at Emma directly. "Honestly. Very good." She looked down at her fork and grew silent again.

205

In the distance, a waterfall of fog spilled over the spires of the city, then seemed to stop and hover, waiting, as was Emma, for the point of the story. Happily ever after wasn't the end of her story and wasn't the story itself. Emma finished her hamburger, ate each and every french fry, drained her beer, ordered another and still she waited. And finally, Vivian looked at her, her amber eyes awash with moisture.

"He—I didn't see him all those years except three times when we found ourselves at the same event. We never spoke. Gene never mentioned it. But someone who didn't know my connection to him mentioned she'd been to a funeral. His wife's, it turned out. She said how bad the widower looked, that he was retiring sooner than expected for reasons of health.

"The last time I saw him, Gene wasn't with me, so I said hello, had a little more time to see him. I tried to hide my shock, he looked so crumply, and grey—his skin, I mean. Not healthy. He was older than I was, but not old enough to look that way. He said his health had been poor, but he was hopeful of a change for the better.

"I didn't ask why. I should have, because then maybe . . . I didn't put together the gray skin, how weak he looked, how slowly he walked up the one step in front of him. Maybe if I'd known . . . But Emma, I didn't suspect a thing. Why would I have? It was fifteen years ago!"

Emma wished she'd ordered coffee instead of beer. It wasn't warm anymore. She wished she were inside anything. Protected in some way she suddenly felt she was not.

"He was on the heart-transplant list. I didn't know. If I had only asked, if I'd known . . . ."

She was off again, lost somewhere. Emma was getting used to this rhythm, and she waited.

"Three days ago," Vivian said in a flat voice, "Gene came

home from the office in a great mood. Buoyant and beaming like something great had happened, and when I asked, he said, 'Vivian, it's over at last.'

"Of course, I had no idea what he was talking about. I thought about his projects, about anything on earth he'd been waiting for—grants, awards, equipment.

"He said, 'Your love affair is what's over. Finally. It took fifteen years, but he's out of your life. And mine. Out of his, too. He's dead. Why the hell would I let him qualify for a new heart after he broke mine? Go ahead, cry for him. Feel whatever you like. Love him. It no longer bothers me a bit. I hear he was a really nice guy.' And he smiled."

Emma shivered.

"If I'd known . . . I would have lied, Emma. I would have said I didn't, I never loved him. But I didn't know and Gene did. And he killed him," Vivian said. "On purpose. Isn't that murder?"

Intentionally killing someone. Yes, of course. Except. She could see Gene's clean healer's hands, could imagine him explaining the complex protocol for deciding who gets transplanted organs and who doesn't. Vivian said he'd been older than she herself was. That would put him near sixty. Borderline age, Emma assumed. In a rarified world, with a procedure as complicated as a heart-transplant, Gene would produce scientific, compassionate, heartfelt, rational and irrefutable arguments. Gene was a physician. The expert in his field. He'd know things nobody else on the jury, in the courtroom, possibly could.

Murder—or speculation. Hysteria. Much too petty an act for the good Dr. Carter whose entire career had been dedicated to saving lives.

And what would be gained? Gene's undeniable lifesaving talents would be rendered useless. Vivian's lover could never return. The situation would never repeat itself.

"I've moved out," Vivian said softly. "It's obvious that those fifteen years were a farce, that just below the calm, there was boiling lava. Fifteen years waiting for revenge; fifteen years of hate—it all came out in that greeting. In less than a minute. I can't live with him anymore, knowing that."

That fury, that murderous rage, that twisted passion. Straight out of a nineteenth century opera. Be careful what you wish for . . .

"What do I do now?" Vivian asked. "What's the right thing to do?"

Nothing would be made better if she went to the authorities. There was nothing they could do. And nothing would be made worse by silence. Nothing had been real for fifteen years. You can't lose what never was.

Emma was glad George wasn't here to witness the dismantling of her carefully calibrated systems. The clear-edged blacks and whites she'd flipped in front of him this morning had muddled into each other to form a non-color. A veil she couldn't see through. "I don't know," she said softly. "I don't know that there's an answer."

"But Emma, you always—I thought you'd—"

"I thought so, too." Emma felt exposed as her absolutes fell away. "But I was wrong." She thought about hearts, their secrets and unknowable mysteries.

In the distance, a foghorn moaned. Emma turned. Fog had swallowed the city until all definition was gone, turned into a fuzzed and featureless wilderness of grey.